HEAR OUR DEFEATS

Laurent Gaudé

HEAR OUR DEFEATS

Translated from the French
by Alison Anderson

Europa
editions

Europa Editions
214 West 29th Street
New York, N.Y. 10001
www.europaeditions.com
info@europaeditions.com

Copyright © 2016 by Editions Actes Sud
First Publication 2019 by Europa Editions

Translation by Alison Anderson
Original title: *Écoutez nos défaites*
Translation copyright © 2019 by Europa Editions

Library of Congress Cataloging in Publication Data is available
ISBN 978-1-60945-500-2

Gaudé, Laurent
Hear Our Defeats

Book design by Emanuele Ragnisco
www.mekkanografici.com

Cover photo © David et Myrtille /Arcangel images

Prepress by Grafica Punto Print – Rome

Printed in the USA

CONTENTS

For Alexandra

At midnight, when suddenly you hear
an invisible procession going by
with exquisite music, voices,
don't mourn your luck that's failing now,
work gone wrong, your plans
all proving deceptive—don't mourn them uselessly:
as one long prepared, and full of courage,
say goodbye to her, to Alexandria who is leaving.
Above all, don't fool yourself, don't say
it was a dream, your ears deceived you:
don't degrade yourself with empty hopes like these.
As one long prepared, and full of courage,
as is right for you who were given this kind of city,
go firmly to the window
and listen with deep emotion,
but not with the whining, the pleas of a coward:
listen—your final pleasure—to the voices,
to the exquisite music of that strange procession,
to say goodbye to her, to the Alexandria you are losing.

—CONSTANTINE CAVAFY
The God Abandons Antony[1]

[1] From *C. P. Cavafy: Collected Poems* translated by Edmund Keeley and Philip Sherrard. Published by Princeton University Press. Copyright © 1972 by Edmund Keeley and Philip Sherrard.

HEAR OUR DEFEATS

I
ZURICH

Everything that accumulates inside us, year after year, without our noticing: the faces we thought we'd forgotten, sensations, ideas we were sure we had fixed so they would endure but which then disappear, return, disappear again, a sign that beyond our consciousness something is alive in us that escapes us but transforms us, everything that moves in that place, advancing darkly, year after year, subconsciously, until one day it surfaces and we are almost seized with fright, because it becomes clear that time has passed and we don't know if it will be possible to live with all these words, all these moments we've experienced and endured, and which end up freighting us, in the way we might refer to a ship. Perhaps that is what we call wisdom: this collection of everything—the sky of Africa, children's promises, car chases through the medina in Tangiers, the face of Shaveen the Kurdish fighter with her long black braids, all of that, the names that were used, the meetings that were arranged, the men who were killed and those who were protected; personally I cannot—wisdom about what? This living collection has not helped me to be more insightful, nor does it weigh upon me, no, it's something else: it sucks me in. More and more often I feel as if my mind is being called upon to explore this inner landscape. The angry crowd on the road between Misrata and Sirte, the fear I try to master but which is welling up inside me, the *café blanc* in Beirut, that very particular sound of heavy weaponry in the outskirts of Benghazi amid a rebel army in full debacle, those moments, all too numerous, when I thought I was done for, and then the intoxication that comes afterwards, mine alone, of realizing I'm still alive, and there's no one who knows or can share that joy, all of that, and the airplanes streaking the sky above Mali on their way to bomb the positions I have just passed on to them, the heat, the strange moments at airports, in transit between two war zones, where I wander around the duty free unable to buy a thing, as if that world, the one of cartons of tax-free cigarettes and pyramids of whisky bottles, was no longer mine. It has all become an entire world that lives and writhes and sometimes, in the middle of the night, brings forth an image: the kids playing at exploding the bullets they've found on the ground in the Shi'ite neighborhoods of Beirut, the softness of an evening in the garden at the ambassador's residence in Bamako, it all calls to me as if from now on another world might be possible, a world to explore and understand, the world I carry inside me. And I feel it today as I walk along the lakefront toward Bellevueplatz: there's something that has changed in me and that I cannot qualify, something growing and sucking me in. I know it cannot be seen yet. I know that a few hours from now, when I am face-to-face with Auguste, I will be the man I have always been: Assem Graieb. Once again I will use this name, it's not mine but I've grown accustomed to it, Assem Graieb, I've been with the agency for over ten years. When I happen to meet the young recruits during an official ceremony at the boulevard Mortier in Paris, they look at me with respect, because although they don't know exactly what I've done, they have seen the list of the territories I've covered: Afghanistan, the Sahel, Libya, Iraq—and that is enough to impress them. Among themselves they refer to me, to Assem Graieb, as "a hunter"—and they are right, I've headed so many operations over the years that I have become a hunter, a killer for the

Republic, constantly on the hunt for new targets. I will always be that man to all of them, because in their eyes Assem Graieb lives on, identical to himself, but personally I know that something is growing inside me, and it is changing me, and someday it may open like a huge gaping internal mouth—and who knows what I will do then . . .

When he asked me where I was from and I said Iraq, I could see in his eyes that he knew my country. Then he looked astonished, and came out with one of those stock phrases I hear when I tell people my nationality: "It's not too hard . . . ?" But he said that just to make it seem innocuous. I could tell. In his gaze, just before that, he knew my country, and that simple word, Iraq, had been enough to take him there. Later on, in the evening, while we were still at the bar, he brought it up again and said, "Where in Iraq?" "Baghdad," I said, and again I saw that merely evoking the name of my city was enough for him to go there in his mind. He made less of an effort to hide it. He remained silent for a long time. And I didn't speak either. Then he gave a gentle smile and I knew we would go up to his room, I knew we would make love. Not just because of Baghdad, but because he had decided to stop acting the man who doesn't know, because the second time he didn't ask one of those questions I get so often: "And do you still go back there . . . ?" No. He just contented himself with the images of that city that were inside him, and he took his time. I immediately knew he was in the military. Or something like that. I told him so. There, in the bar. Before he took me gently by the hand, the way a boy in high school does when he wants to slip away from the classroom with his sweetheart to find somewhere more discreet. In that room where we could see the Limmat flowing past, and where we were now the last patrons, I said, "You're in the military, aren't you." And he laughed. He didn't deny it. He even said, "Is it that

obvious . . . ?" Then what might have been a joke: "So I'll
have to change jobs." I knew because he agreed, all evening,
not to hide anything. And I didn't ask any questions he couldn't
have answered. He smiled when I said "military." He took
some time to think about the landscapes of Iraq that he carried inside him when I said "Baghdad." He didn't lie. So I followed him, and we went upstairs. I stumbled, I think, in the
corridor on the fourth floor. The thick carpet muffled the
sound but we laughed. I'd had a lot to drink. So had he. I had
to put my hand in front of my mouth. I was carrying one of
my shoes in the other hand. I was walking lopsidedly and he
was laughing. That hand of his, holding me by the waist, I
loved it right from the start. I don't know how long I've been
meeting men in hotel bars. In Paris. Geneva. New York. He
wasn't the first. I started after I split up with Marwan. Now
and again one of them is surprised. That I'm an Iraqi woman.
As if that should stop the body from desiring, should stop
"the despair need to love." Marwan liked to quote Éluard.
That is one thing of his I have kept. And a liking for sex, too,
perhaps . . . I remember how when we made love in
Alexandria in that apartment he had rented, overlooking the
sea, we were so eager to make the most of those hours he had
stolen from his life, from his wife, from Cairo, from the
museum . . . I would have Marwan all to myself, just a little,
for a few hours a month, which might add up to a few days a
year . . . I loved those moments. I thought I was free. Poetry,
love, and meals at odd times, in the street, at a sidewalk café
in the port, at a time when others are having their siesta or
drinking a coffee. I loved all that. Then came solitude, always.
And waiting. Until he left me. It took me by surprise. I was
convinced I'd be the one to leave. I remember that day: he
arrived late, frowning. I didn't immediately notice that there'd
be no holding one another, no lovers' walks, that there would
be only a quick, curt exchange, and that this time Marwan had

come in order to go away for good. It was afterwards, yes, it must have been, that I began to say yes to men in hotels.

The air is cool, invigorating. I should have walked briskly, the way I so often have on similar occasions. I am about to meet Auguste, my branch chief. He will be assigning a new mission. It's all starting up again. I will be Assem Graieb, or someone else. I will be a Frenchman of Algerian, or Tunisian, or Libyan origin. So many lives, in succession, and danger, always, making them intense. But I am walking slowly, and at this moment my mind is filled with the little cries of excitement the chess player at the Lindenhof kept making. Why am I thinking about him again? I don't know. I watched him yesterday for a long time. More than an hour. I sat there on a bench by these two huge chessboards the city of Zurich set up in a garden overlooking the town, and you can see the Limmat flowing from there, just as Roman soldiers would have seen it. I watched the man as he wiggled this way and that, suppressing his madness so that he could play and not lose the thread of the game. I stayed for a long time and eventually I heard the others say his name, his successive opponents, for there were many of them—students, notables, pensioners—and they all ended up handing on their place, vexed at having lost so quickly: Ferruccio der Verrückte. For hours, yes, as if I were hypnotized, I observed the twitching of his shoulders, the grimace of his mouth, the way he had of raising his eyebrows and suddenly leaning forward as if someone had punched him in the stomach. He was crazy, Ferruccio, and couldn't sit still, he would take great strides along the ground on the chessboard or fiddle with the wooden pieces, which were knee high, as if he were commanding a living army. Ferruccio: he's the one I can hear as I walk along. And I am also thinking about the hotel room I have just left behind me, bathed in a lovely morning light, with the bed and its rumpled sheets, the room she left before me. And it is only now, by the banks of the Limmat, as I am coming to the last bridge before the lake, that I remember I told her to meet me there, on the Bellevueplatz, the same place I am supposed to meet Auguste so he can introduce me to our American contact, but one hour earlier, and I cannot think why I did that, why I made that appointment with her. In my mind Ferruccio is still pacing back and forth, turning, swallowing his adversary's pieces, making those shrill little cries, and there's no way of knowing which he dreads more, defeat, or the solitude that will follow his victory, when the notable or the student, as vexed as all those who went before, will walk away, giving a wave of helplessness, conceding that yes, Ferruccio was better, and leaving him there, unvanquished but alone. He plays well, very well. He is lively and farsighted, but on his face there is always an anxiousness that contorts his features, as if he were sorry to be winning, as if he hoped someone would beat him at last so it would calm the tics that eat away at him and appease the inner commotion he tries so hard to contain. Unless what he is actually hoping for is a game that will never end, something that will absorb him utterly and wholly, then at last the world would be dismissed and he, the madman, will find relief. All that remains will be the chess pieces, the diagonals, the advances, the traps, the sacrifices, pure intelligence, and Ferruccio der Verrückte, the man who plays with his shirttail hanging out, or even bare-chested sometimes, the man who has a thick beard and talks to himself, even insulting himself, will no longer exist. There will be nothing but the intensity of this thing that is built by two players, something that no longer resembles combat but is, rather, the search for a form of perfection, like a scientific discovery: the never-ending chess match, the one for which the game was conceived. I think again of Mariam, whom I met yesterday, and the night we spent together, with the tacit agreement that we would not ask each other who we really are, our occupations, our lives; that our first names, Assem and Mariam, and our two bodies would suffice. Why did I arrange to meet her this morning? I still see her thick black hair, smooth and shining in the half-light. I see her lips, the eager, almost greedy way she spoke when we were in the bar, and then how they parted, later, with delight, in that room overlooking the calm waters of the river, to let out a sigh of rapture—a moment of a purity that makes up for everything: the wandering, the fatigue. Her parted lips, letting out the joyful, instantaneous breath of sexual pleasure, the bliss of oblivion. And above all I remember now how I felt and what I can only refer to as a strange, new shyness. How I hesitated when the moment came to get undressed: did she notice? I don't think so. Or rather, she didn't mind, she could see the cracks and tears on my body but it didn't surprise her. She accepted it, as she accepted doubt, and a certain mental lassitude. We approached each other without embarrassment, with respect. And perhaps, in the end, that is what compelled me to make that appointment with her this morning. I can't see any other explanation. So, Ferruccio, the madman of the Lindenplatz, is laughing at me, because he alone understands that something has been born that will take me far beyond the lands where for ten years France has been sending me to kill or protect, even when I could never be sure whether we were winning or losing, because I always had to start over, there were always new missions in the field and new enemies to slay, always new zones of influence to maintain or new strategic points to control, and Ferruccio is laughing because he knows, *he knows*, that when the darkness falls, when the last adversary has been crushed, that's when the worst time begins, because that's when you have to accept your return to your own tics and torments.

From far away he can hear the sound of the helicopter, and he cannot tell whether it is coming from beyond the mountains or the depths of his memory. The sound of blades grows louder until it drowns out everything. The wind is whipping his face. At that moment he thinks of all the helicopters he has taken, all those flights, during the day, at night . . . He hears the approaching helicopter and never mind if he cannot open his eyes, he knows that its arrival will free him from threat, from blows, that the aircraft will cover him with a protective shadow. But what if it doesn't reach him? Maybe it will come too late or will have to fly off again, unable to land in this hostile city, making a huge curve in the sky then moving off into space? It hardly matters. Just knowing that it came, that someone sent this aircraft to get him, is comfort enough and it fills him with peace. He thinks of all the helicopters he has left, jumping out onto the hills of faraway countries in the middle of the night, he thinks of how he approached the houses he was going to violate along with the men who came with him, breaking down doors, roughly shoving aside the drowsy women who screamed in stupor, how they turned a deaf ear to everything around them, the faces, the shouts, the entreaties, searching in the night for a man who always gave himself up in the end, and all those times when it was his hands that did the beating. He remembers all those night flights when he was like a silent raptor with night vision, erupting in lives that didn't expect him and vanishing before anyone could really react. He has taken so many helicopters. And he hears this one without being able to determine whether it really is getting closer, until he hears the voice, "Sullivan . . . ?" constantly saying his name, "Sullivan . . . ?" and adding a few words that he recognizes because he has said them himself in other countries, at other times, when it was his turn to go to the assistance of suffering bodies, the words you say to tell them to hang on, that everything will be all right, they're going to take you home, the words to emphasize that need to hold on . . . What does he want to hold on to? "Sullivan . . . ?" And that name they throw at him, over and over, as if they didn't want to let him close his eyes, as if he didn't have the right to give up. "Sullivan . . . ?", and so he eventually says "yes," not with his lips—no, he can't do that anymore—not in an audible, articulate way, he no longer has the strength, but he says "yes" in his mind and immediately wishes he hadn't, as if he had yielded to convenience, as if he hasn't been up to the gravity of the moment, when he could have stayed in the burning village and died there, but it's too late, in his soul he has said "yes" and there are arms bearing him away, carrying him, dragging him to the helicopter and its promises, with the dull sound of its engine and the power of its blades, to get him out of that place that should have been his grave.

It was different somehow, with that man at the Zum Storchen hotel who said his name was Assem. I woke up in the middle of the night. I felt good. I let the sweet atmosphere of the room enfold me. I thought he was asleep at my side; I was wrong. He must have felt from the movement of my body that I was awake. Without moving, in a soft voice, he asked me to tell him about my profession, to tell him an archeologist's story. I thought of Mariette Pasha. Because of the Bes statue, in all likelihood. Had I already decided, at that point, what to do with it? I don't think so. But Mariette Pasha had come in the room and I could sense that Assem was all ears. I told him about the day in Abydos when the French archeologist showed his workers where they should dig. I told him how the men started digging and were amazed when they came upon the relics. And I told him, in that calm night that was happy like a an unexpected respite in our lives, how a worker asked Mariette how he knew they were there. And Mariette Pasha answered: "I knew because I'm three thousand years old." Assem listened. He didn't laugh. As a rule, when I tell this story, people laugh, they think it's just some sort of witty remark. But Asssem didn't. He didn't laugh because he is like me: he knows it's true. And he asked who Mariette Pasha was. So I told him a little about this pioneer of modern archeology. I told him about the discovery of the Serapeum. "What's the Serapeum?" I explained that it was a tomb for the bulls of Apis. This intrigued him. "The bulls of Apis?" So I gave him more: the priest designated a sacred bull, with a black coat and a white upside-down triangle on its forehead. I told him about the animal's long procession down the banks of the Nile and how the men everywhere would bow down before it. I told him how whenever an Apis bull died there were seventy days of mourning, and the creature was embalmed and then buried in the temple where all the bulls were buried one after the other, generation after generation, and the priests were already looking for the reincarnation of the bull that had just died. "All that over a bull?" he said, admiringly. Yes. And Mariette Pasha found the spot. Before anyone. Without even knowing yet that after this his life would never be the same and he would be forever bound to Egypt—this little man from Boulogne-sur-Mer who would end up a pasha and be buried in the museum at Bulaq. The difficulties with the digs. The waiting, to obtain the legendary firman that would grant him permission to dig, and the day when they could at last open the door they had managed to free from the sand. I told him how a column of blue vapor had risen from the open door, "as if from the mouth of a volcano," says Mariette in his writings. For four hours the tomb exhaled the air that had been imprisoned there for centuries. I see Assem closing his eyes, imagining the scene. Deeper in, in the burial chamber, Mariette discovered not only the sarcophagi of the bulls but also, on the ground, the shape of a foot in the dust. The last priest to leave the chamber before closing the door. The shape of his foot, frozen in the dust, motionless for thirty centuries. And what should have been fragile, what should have been erased by the first gust of wind, had survived it all—the wars, the famines, the decline of civilizations, the upheavals of the world. I tell him all this. And I know from the intensity of his silence that he thinks as I do, both that it is extraordinary and also that in opening the door, in letting the air out and allowing the footprint to disappear, there has been a sort of violation that could reduce you to tears. At the end, when I fell silent, I thought he wasn't going to say anything, that he must be a bit embarrassed, maybe I'd gone on too long, it was strange to be evoking Mariette Pasha and the sacred bulls of Egypt when we were lying there naked side by side, but there was no embarrassment. He didn't say anything for a while, as if to let the images of the distant past live a little longer, the banks of the Nile, the crowd on its knees, the chosen bull entering the temple—then he too began to talk. He just recited a few lines of poetry. I remember. It was at that point, I think, that I knew what I was going to do. He said, "Body, remember, not only how much you have been loved, not only the beds on which you have lain, but also the eyes that shone, the voices that trembled, with desires for you . . . " That was his way of responding to the bulls of Apis, to give me something in exchange. He added the poet's name: Cavafy. I wept, quietly. It was as if he had guessed. Marwan. Alexandria. It was as if he knew about the disease that is inside me, and how tired I am, sometimes, of this life of struggle. So I wept, yes, and he did not try to comfort me, he knew it was better that way, that the crying was cleansing me of something I could not talk about. "Body, remember, not only how much you have been loved . . . " That was when I knew that I would love this man, I knew that he was giving me Cavafy's words because of a presentiment—through some inexplicable insight—that they would do me good, and that was when I knew I would give him the Bes statue I have had for so long without telling anyone, because in that moment I had met someone who, like me, was three thousand years old.

Could it be that four thirty in the morning on April 12, 1861, was the moment of his resurrection? Could it be that when young Beauregard, the Confederate Army general, ordered his artillery to open fire at Fort Sumter, where Robert Anderson was entrenched with his Union soldiers, that precise moment with its multitude of deaths, even if no one would die in the next thirty-four hours, the thirty-four hours of pounding it took to reduce the fort to rubble, the thirty-four hours for the South to proclaim its deep, joyful secession, a brief period of liberation and defiance as incarnated by the confrontation between young Beauregard and the man who had been his instructor at West Point—the very same Robert Anderson who, a few years earlier, had been so impressed by the young Confederate's talent that he had offered him a post as his assistant—could it be that when that shot was fired, when the stone was shattered, this great eructation of pleasure was, for Ulysses S. Grant, a moment of resurrection? He can feel it. He reads and rereads the article in the little Illinois newspaper his father left on the table there in the overpowering smell of the tannery, and he knows this is his chance. Thirty-four hours of shooting and at the end, Anderson raising the white flag, and Beauregard smiling, the joyful cheers of the entire population of the South. Fort Sumter has fallen. And in Mississippi and Louisiana and South Carolina they are dancing for joy. That newly elected president by the name of Lincoln, no one knows him, and he won't be theirs. Let the North have him! Ulysses Grant reads and rereads the article just to feel the slap. Because that is precisely what Beauregard has done with his artillery: he has given Lincoln, and all of Washington along with him, a slap in the face. A slap in the face, too, to old General Scott, the hero of the Mexican wars, and to all the Yankees. Ulysses Grant wants a drink. It would do him good. Even if it is only ten o'clock in the morning. That never stopped him from drinking. Until he collapsed, even. He can't hold his liquor, never could. But isn't that the very reason you drink? To blow your brains out with shots of scotch. He would very much like to have a glass or two right now, so his hand would stop trembling, and to ease the sting of humiliation. But he knows he won't. Because Beauregard's artillerymen have just set him free. A wreck. That's what he was until now. A man of a thousand wasted lives. Alcohol forced him out of the army. What could he do? Stay in that isolated posting in the north of California, where the slow passage of days seemed to delight in tormenting him, and where there was nothing to do but drink, and watch the procession of clouds in the sky, reminiscing about the fear he'd known at Molino del Rey? He'd tried. Seven lives. Farmer. Real estate agent. Firewood dealer. A wreck. He couldn't do it. The bottle was always better. He had always known he'd be condemned to this: the self-hatred, the spectacle of his mediocrity constantly there before him, his shame in the eyes of his wife, who knows she'll have to raise their four children on her own, and he loves her for this, for her resilience, but it hasn't been enough to make the bottle go away. Only the shells at Fort Sumter can do that. He could tell, right away. He has been waiting for so long. What a sweet feeling . . . No slap has ever been sweeter. So he reads the article again, until his cheeks are flushed. He tries to picture Robert Anderson, head bowed, emerging from the rubble with his men, and the cries of joy everywhere that make Beauregard smile with satisfaction. This, yes, this is strong enough to make him forego the drink. This, he can tell, will sweep away his father's tannery, where he came back to work for lack of anything better, it will sweep away the days of depression, the painful memories of Chapultepec. He will become a warrior again, and so much the better, because perhaps he is only ever really himself when he's in uniform. Right down to his name, which the army modified in error: Ulysses S. Grant, which he prefers to his real name, Hiram Ulysses Grant, because the latter is the name of a failed life, of trades where he did not earn a penny, the name of the bottle rolling under the chair where he has fallen asleep, it's the name of his wife's gaze, not reproachful but disappointed, it's the name of a long life that is going to wear him out, so yes, Ulysses S. Grant, he'll always like that better. And may Beauregard go on smiling, wherever he is. May Jefferson Davis make all the declarations he likes, may Virginia continue to hesitate, then join the camp of the Confederates, that's fine, it's in need of a few slaps. Only anger will save him from boredom. And he can sense, now, that the defeat at Fort Sumter is an opportunity, one of those that come along only once in a lifetime, and it will save him from disaster.

Today, he must resign himself to dying. And yet, everything is so beautiful . . . His army occupies the hill overlooking Maychew plain, a huge crowd, led by the princes of Ethiopia, all of them, like him, descendants of the heroes of Adwa, the glorious warriors who defeated Italy: Menelik II, Taytu Betul, Mengesha Yohannes. Today every fighter is thinking of that as they hurry through the colorful crowd. They invoke the spirit of their ancestors and hope to prove themselves as brave as they were. They beat their chests, and encourage each other, hair disheveled, beards unshaven. They have braided their hair and are covered with jewels. They move forward in their brightly colored clothing. None of them are wearing uniforms. They have armed themselves with iron, occasionally guns or knives. They let the rage of war well up and again hope that this will be the day of their great victory. Haile Selassie gazes out at the still-swelling crowd of people. For months everything has been converging toward this place, this day. It is as if all his efforts since the beginning of the war have had no other purpose than to end in this battle. It was to reach this moment that on last October 3 at eleven A.M., to the sound of the kitet, he launched the call from the steps of his palace for a general mobilization, and throughout the country the beating of drums proclaimed war. It is for this moment that a dense, spontaneous crowd of warriors, men of all ages, has swarmed toward Addis Ababa. Since the Italians' very first attack, at Walwal, this great final battle has already been in preparation. Mussolini wants his revenge. He only sent this expeditionary corps under the command of Marshal Badoglio in order to wipe away the affront of Adwa and retake Ethiopia. And today everything is ready. His warriors are massed there before him. They are waiting for his signal to rush onto the plain and rout the enemy. He holds himself straight, between Ras Desta and Ras Kassa. He is calm. He is taking his time to study everything. Soon the rush will come, and the combat. Soon the blood. One last time he says the name to himself, Maychew. He does not address those who surround him because he dares tell no one what he truly thinks: that they have come here, to Maychew, to die.

I am sitting on the Bellevueplatz in the concrete kiosk; there's a continuous bench all around it to provide seating for people who are waiting for the tram on rainy days or for those who, like me, would just like to sit here and gaze at the comings and goings in the street. I am slowly drinking the coffee I bought, to go, at the bar next to the kiosk where the tickets are sold. The trams pass each other, stop, set off again, number 5, number 7 . . . On they go, on their continuous gliding route. Some will go along the lake, others cross the bridge. Men and women alight. The city grows livelier. Everyone going about their daily life: shopping, picking up the children, meeting a friend. I no longer belong to that life. Where are they all going with such a determined air? Can they actually believe in this life, be truly a part of it? Something in me has shifted. It's imperceptible, but I can feel it. I know that I shouldn't be thinking about anything besides my meeting with Auguste, I should be giving it my full concentration, but I just can't seem to. Soon he will tell me my next destination. We will sip our ristretti calmly, and Auguste will give me a certain amount of information. I can't focus on it. I keep seeing Mariam's thick hair shining in the night. I see her bare shoulders and the gentle movements of her hands. I continue to watch the trams go by. The coffee is getting cold in the little paper cup I'm holding in the palm of my hand. Is this a sign I'm getting old? There's this feeling of an imperceptible rift, it's distancing me from things, it leaves me feeling not as tense, not as sharp, and more and more often I find myself observing the world as if it were a stage set. Perhaps I made an appointment with the woman solely to leave myself the possibility that something might happen before my appointment with Auguste, before the French Republic once again grabs hold of me and gives me a new name, a mission, a zone of operations. Is that what I want? To delay the moment when the man who is my superior, whom I've known for years but have always called Auguste, in the full knowledge that Auguste is not his real name, will give me an envelope containing—as they all have for ten years now—plane tickets, a contact in a faraway city, and precise instructions. I wonder if this is not what I hoped for last night, when I told Mariam I would be at Bellevueplatz at ten o'clock: to escape from who I am.

Alive. He made me feel alive. I hadn't felt that way in such a long time. So when he told me to meet him at Bellevueplatz at ten o'clock I didn't reply, but I knew already that I would go. I left the hotel and walked out into the cool morning air of the waking city. I crossed the Bellevue bridge and then went along the eastern riverbank. I felt like breathing in whole lungfuls of that air. Alive. Yes. In spite of the disease lurking inside me, the disease they told me about as they scrutinized my blood work, with that serious, concentrated expression, the disease that has called for further tests, that will require a specialist and certain protocols, the disease I finally saw on an X-ray they waved in front of me. But even then it was still abstract. How can I believe that an opaque spot could have the slightest influence on my life? How can I even believe that what was on the X-ray, lying flat on a backlit surface, had anything whatsoever to do with me? Often, now, I try to listen to myself. In the evening. I breathe more softly, and listen carefully in hopes that I will be able to hear from inside my body what it is that is eating away at me and feeding on my strength in order to grow. This man, with the pleasure he gave me and the close way he listened while I was talking about the Serapeum and Mariette Pasha, he made me forget my inner enemy. That is not why I am going to the appointment, not out of gratitude, or desire, but because I could see his shortcomings. He didn't hide. A man perched on the edge of an abyss. I felt he was going to disappear and it seemed to me that there should be someone there to witness the moment he left himself. I can tell he is leaving for a place you don't return from, or if you do, you are so changed that it is impossible to say whether you have truly come back. I board the tram, and it's not because of the package I slipped into his bag before dawn, when he was still sleeping. I doubt he's found it yet. I board the tram but I won't tell him anything about the Bes statue I tucked at the bottom of his suitcase between two shirts, with a little note written in the dawn light; I tried not to make any noise. Maybe he won't understand just what the statue represents? Maybe our paths will never cross again, but I know it was the right thing to do. The statue was made to be passed on. From hand to hand, century to century.

The defeat has come. Do the others not see it? Cruel, ravenous defeat, irremediable. They cannot escape it. Is he the only one who can feel it? The generals are handing a little pair of binoculars back and forth, counting the Italian troops and the Eritrean regiments over and over. Sometimes they hand him the binoculars as well so he too can evaluate the situation, but he doesn't. He is the emperor of them all, king of kings, Haile Selassie, he is sure of their defeat but what good would it do to tell them? He keeps his legendary calm, saying nothing, no words of fear or haste. He is time remaining impassive, the eyes that see what shall be. His men gaze at him, a little man in his impeccable uniform, the only man wearing one. The others, all the others, are shaggy, with blankets over their shoulders, jewelry around their necks and in their ears, on their wrists, and knives in their belts. He says nothing. He was against this battle. What good does it do to count the enemy's numbers again and again? They are going to die today. He knows it. The Italians may not be as numerous, but Ras Desta and Ras Kassa are wrong to see this as a good sign, to see it as a reason for hope regarding the outcome of the battle. The only thing that is certain is that the Italians are going to crush them. He has known this ever since they imposed the blockade and he didn't know how to break it. Neither France nor Britain would give way. He tried everything, in vain. And today he knows he has no weapons. Only one 75mm cannon, given to him by the Maréchal Franchet d'Espèry on behalf of a hypocritical French nation on the day of his coronation. Just one cannon. And not a single fighter plane. His men are brave, yes, but they march on foot or on the backs of mules, so they are going to lose. For a while he thought that the weapons Hitler had agreed to sell him would be enough to break the blockade, but the rifles arrived in small, scattered shipments and were lost in the vast country . . . He has no armaments. The only war he might have envisaged, and which might have led to victory after months or years of fighting, was a guerrilla war. Let the enemy come in, take possession of the country, then harass them, wear them out, ruin them bit by bit in a war at the end of the world, a war they would eventually abandon because it was costing too much. That is what he should have done. But he is Haile Selassie, king of kings, prisoner of his own self, and he could not. His generals told him: "A king doesn't fight a guerrilla war, like some *shifta*,"[2] and it sounded like a slap in the face. A king fights a proper war. And if he is meant to lose, the best thing is for him to die on the battlefield. That is what lies ahead for them, all of them, his sons-in-law, his warriors, all his subjects put together: they will die in one last, great battle. A head-on collision, pointless and bloody, but History will remember it. It cannot be any other way. So what does it matter, the movement of enemy troops, the number of planes Mussolini unleashes in the sky over Ethiopia: he knows that from now on he will be living in chaos, and nothing else.

The tram glides along the river. I allow the city to unfold before my eyes, all the way to the Bellevueplatz. When it stops, I don't get off. Why should I? I look out the window. I'm looking for him. All we need is to see each other, one more time. All I need is for him to catch a glimpse of me, to see that I came, that I understood he needed someone to say goodbye to him today. All we need is a few seconds that will suddenly make our encounter something more than a night of sex in a hotel room, something more than all those nights when I kissed men I would never see again. All I need is for him to see me. I'm going to go back to my life, to my work at the British Museum, my meetings with UNESCO, my expert's reports for Interpol, my life as an archeologist chasing after a multitude of stolen artifacts. I will go back to my nights of deep fear, those moments when I cannot help but think about my illness, the spot that is growing, the ugliness of my body as it begins

[2] Bandit.

to disintegrate (how soon? A year? Two?) . . . I will go back to all that, but knowing I have this vision I can hold before me, and it will do me good, it will help to assuage the terror and the melancholy. I will have this man, on the Bellevueplatz, the image of this man, in the cool morning, and the line of poetry he gave me, as if he knew: "Body, remember, not only how much you have been loved . . . "

Sweet moments. I could spend the entire day here. As every tram stops, out spills a small crowd of men and woman, all rushing to get out, all in a hurry. For a few seconds they surround me then they scatter and the tram goes on its way, until the next one comes to immerse me again in the busyness of humankind. I drink my coffee slowly. I don't have much time left before I will have to stand up, cross the street, and go into the building across the way, where Auguste is surely already waiting for me with France, orders, faraway countries and the names of men to kill.

And then all of a sudden, just as I am about to get up, her face appears there in front of me, in the tram. She is at the window, staring out at me. This is why she came, I can tell. She won't get off. She is going to stay there at the back of the tram, facing the window. I stand up, take a few steps toward her, why, I don't know . . . Then the tram gives an initial judder to set off again, making that shrill little sound so that pedestrians will get off the rails, and then slowly she raises her hand, in a sort of gesture—of what? And we gaze at each other again, until the tram is completely out of sight. She didn't get off. Why would she have? To come and drink a coffee? Have a talk? Only for us to constantly bump up against the lives we cannot share, because it would take too long, be too fastidious, because the pleasure of being together stems precisely from the fact that we have managed to avoid all of that? She came so we could look at each other, long and slow . . . She has understood that I cannot give more than that. Her voice, the story of the bulls of Apis, the long column of blue smoke emerging from the mouth of the tomb for four hours, the beauty of her body, it all inhabits me again. To say farewell, that is why she came. Farewell, yes, she has said as much with her hand, that vague gesture, her two big eyes that seem to have seen everything and fear nothing, farewell, now I know for certain that everything can begin.

And then, at that very moment, everything begins. He can tell. He sees the soldier running toward him down the central path of the encampment, past the tents that have been pitched there for eight months, and as he runs past, the other soldiers come out, look up, freeze. They all sense that something is about to happen, that the news the running soldier has brought to Hannibal is important. He remains motionless, ready to receive the news, there among his people, these rough men who have already fought the Olcades, the Vaccaei, and the Carpetani to unify Hispania, until finally the messenger speaks: Saguntum has fallen. There it is: the siege of the city is reaching its end. Eight months of slow, patient strangulation, to reach this day. Everything begins now. Crossing the Strait of Gibraltar was nothing. The land was so close. There was no border to cross and the ships landed easily. Crossing the Pyrenees will be nothing, either. Even if the mountains are high, there are passes, and they will find them. They will get help from the local population, and if they are tight-lipped, they will burn their feet until they talk. No, it is with the fall of Saguntum that everything begins. And Rome, perhaps, does not yet know this. Rome, so reluctant to come to the help of this city, her ally. Rome, not at all wary of this man, because they know only the name of his father, Hamilcar, who ventured as far as Sicily on pirate raids, but they are about to learn the names of his sons: Hannibal, Hasdrubal, and Mago. Rome will learn those names and she will weep and tremble and wake at night, and eventually she will understand that she is much in need of allies and that it was a mistake not to offer to help Saguntum. But for the time being, Rome does not know. Hannibal alone has received the news: Saguntum has fallen. The march can begin. He will leave Hasdrubal to reign over Hispania, and he will cross the Pyrenees. All around him the soldiers are shouting with joy. And the people everywhere will soon learn that Saguntum could not count on Rome's help. Alliances will unravel. That is what is needed: for Rome to face them on her own, and then they will devour her. Now the soldiers regroup and surround him, forming a dense crowd. The rebels from the Balearic Islands, who go around with their chests bound in leather straps; the Numidian horsemen, who are the craziest, the bravest; the Iberian foot soldiers he managed to rally to his army; the Libyans who play their citharas with a smile on their faces: they all acclaim him, in their own language, with their heavy, cutthroat joy. For the first time they sense that the young man who is there in front of them and whom they have promised to obey is not some little warlord, but a conqueror, that what they will be called on to take part in will not be a series of mercenary raids, but a page of History, because this is how History is written—who could ever doubt it?—with a weapon in one's fist, in serried ranks around three brothers. And what they may be sensing at this moment is the inspiration of Alexander the Great, because they know they are about to set off down endless roads, the way Alexander did with his armies, they are about to pursue conquests that no one could ever have imagined before they did, and so they cheer, Hannibal, Hannibal . . . They can sense that they are about to be penetrated by History, whether they are dead or alive, glorious or crushed. They know they are about to begin their march, Hannibal . . . Hannibal . . . and that the world will never be the same . . .

The helicopter lifts up and away from Kalafgan. Inside, the soldiers are restless, cannot stop talking. He would like to ask them to be quiet. He hears them say that his pulse is getting weaker, that he has lost a lot of blood. He hears them referring to the wound in his leg and his face distorted by blows. He can feel them handling him. He cannot tell whether he is still lying flat on the floor of the helicopter or whether they have hoisted him onto a stretcher, just as he cannot tell whether they have already jabbed his arm with a dose to ease the pain and calm his body. He can feel the thick warm contact of his own blood. On his neck. On his leg. He would like to tell them to be quiet and leave him alone, not that he wants to die, he thinks he will live, that's the way it is, but he would still like to have time to hear the women weeping the way mourning mothers have wept for centuries, with powerful sobs in their throats preventing all speech, as if they were animals, bundles of flesh from which some part had been recently amputated. He wants to listen carefully and hear that chant because it feels as if it is up to him to echo it. He is the one who should be rising in the sky and drowning out the sound of the blades, and he knows that with each passing second the women will be farther and farther away. They must already be tiny, far away, almost invisible, still weeping, but to no one but themselves, weeping over the children they will not find, who only a few seconds ago were playing in the schoolyard and are now buried under the rubble. He would like to hear their voices and perhaps give the men of Kalafgan the chance to throw stones, to shoot, even, if they have weapons, and never mind if they damage the helicopter or destroy it, never mind if it means dying there, that would be the closest thing to justice. There is something repulsive about the ease with which he is getting away. He wants to confront the women again, and their hatred, why not . . . The blows, the spitting, it is already all so far away, and will never come again—that scene, as he saw it only a few minutes ago, is vanishing, the flames are slowly dying, the stones grow cold, the rubble is turned over, dug through, and body parts are found and buried, piously. Soon the women will weep only when night comes for them. The scene fades, is already almost completely erased, and he stays here, with his ravaged body, with the blood sticking to his trousers, his eyes swollen from the beatings, his lips split. It's so strange . . . Only a few minutes ago he was running through the streets of Kalafgan, sheltering his face with his arms to try to fend off the blows, and it seemed the voices around him would never let him go. And now it is all so far away. He remembers the instant when everything in him surrendered, when the blood in his eye, in his mouth, was no longer of any importance. He remembers the moment when he accepted death, and he did so without hatred, probably because of the women's weeping, or because he has killed too often not to recognize his enemy's right to take his life. He remembers that instant and yet the men surrounding him are saying that name he thought he no longer needed: "Sullivan?", and so he has taken refuge in a place where he cannot be reached, where knowing whether he is bleeding or not doesn't matter anymore, where knowing whether he will ever use his leg again does not worry him, a place above everything, where the helicopter is flying gracefully through the sky and the chant of the weeping women still has time to resonate, because it is the only thing, in this moment, that the world must hear: the grief of the vanquished mothers.

II
ARGOS

A re you ready to go?" He hadn't heard his uncle's voice in a long time. The memory resurfaced all of a sudden, as if it had been lurking there in some corner of his memory, just waiting for the time and the opportunity, as if, above all, all those words from the past had decided to remind him of their existence in the form of an enigma that, for the time being, he didn't understand at all but which, he could tell, was going to lead him to a point where any man would question his own certainties. The taxi is driving slowly toward Charles de Gaulle airport. The sky is clear. He watches the city he is about to leave unfolding before his eyes. "Are you ready to go?" He remembers the day he was asked this question. The day before his first mission. His uncle had invited him over for dinner. They had talked about poetry and politics. The old man had a mischievous air about him when he talked about all the upheavals in the world, as if, unlike others who saw only chaos, he actually managed to find meaning in all the international tension and unrest and tragedy. And then, during dessert, there in the half-empty restaurant, he had put his question to Assem. At first Assem had answered somewhat gullibly, with a frank "yes." Then the old man took his time. That wasn't what he was referring to. "Do you remember Agamemnon?" he asked. And Assem can still hear his voice as if his old uncle were sitting there with him in the taxi that is now on the A1 northbound freeway. How is it that today, suddenly, he remembers that conversation, and so clearly? If someone had asked him yesterday whether he recalled a single word he exchanged with his uncle ten years ago in that little restaurant in the 14th arrondissement, he would probably have said no, but this morning it's all coming back to him, and in detail. Where had those images, those scenes been hiding? Where in his memory were they, initially inaccessible then surfacing with the clarity of a recent event? The old man had talked about Mycenae. Yes. He remembers. It's as if the further in he ventures, the better his recall. "Everyone knows about the Trojan War, but you'd think no one has ever really thought about it properly . . . What does the myth tell us?" He had let his uncle talk, and the old man took his time. He had evoked the long days without wind. The Achaeans with a worried, impatient expression on their faces. The days went by and the wind did not rise. It was becoming obvious that the gods refused to let them leave. Every morning in Mycenae the men hurried to the highest point at the top of the city, near the palace walls, and stared at the mountains all around them, trying to feel even the slightest breeze on their faces, but there was nothing . . . The tension was rising. What did the gods want? And then came the sacrifice of Iphigenia. Agamemnon leading his daughter to the altar, and then she, to the stupefaction of all the warriors gathered there, took her own life. The wind, a few seconds later, like a response from the heavens; the wind blowing down from the mountains, causing the flags to snap. The old man spoke excitedly. Assem remembers how it was. How there was no one left in the restaurant, and they were alone just the two of them, with Mycenae. The Achaeans were shouting for joy. The Achaeans made ready to board their ships. All the men were converging onto the plain of Argos. A great procession emptied the city of Mycenae. Everyone was celebrating the departure. It wouldn't be long until the warriors returned covered in gold. It wouldn't be long until Menelaus's honor was avenged. "You understand what the myth is saying?" He would give anything to hear his uncle's voice again, there at his side. How he had loved his uncle, the man who had raised him. He didn't know how to reply, so the old professor from Sciences Po continued his story. According to the myth, before they had even made landfall in Asia Minor, before they could even see the walls of Ilium, Agamemnon had lost. He had had to kill his daughter. What victory could be worth such a sacrifice? Even if he managed to raze Troy to the ground, even if he crushed his enemies and reigned for centuries, had he not been defeated right from the start? "Are you ready to go?" That was what his uncle had asked. And now he understands better. You do not go into battle with the hope of returning intact. "Remember Mycenae . . . " Already upon departure, blood and mourning. Already upon departure you must accept the fact that you will be cut off from what is dearest to you. Already upon departure you can be sure there will be no complete, joyful victory. Now, in the back seat of his taxi, he thinks of the wind. The wind of Mycenae, synonym of death. He thinks of those warriors boarding their ships, eager for a fight, who failed to notice that something had already been lost, there behind them. His uncle was right. He has experienced it so often. With every mission he has left a part of himself behind. So now, in the back of his taxi, he wonders what part of himself, this time, he will have to sacrifice to the wind.

She arrived in Paris that very morning. She feels more and more like leaving London and moving here. She would have to go on traveling back and forth between the British Museum and UNESCO, but she would like to try. Perhaps the memory of her conversations with Marwan has something to do with it . . .

When she steps into her little office at UNESCO, she already knows she won't be staying there. Two days from now she has to be in Baghdad. The Iraqi president has decided to reopen the National Museum, which has been closed for years. Sending a powerful signal. To show that Iraq is getting back on its feet, reclaiming its history. The director of UNESCO will be going, and she has been called on to go with her. She won't have time to enjoy Paris, or any time to think about her trip to Zurich and the man she met there. Her life is made up of moments like this, quick, intense, breathless. She feels a wave of enthusiasm: the museum is going to reopen. For years she's been hunting down stolen artifacts, all over the world. It's a stubborn, patient occupation, and she has applied herself to it with a vengeance. She recalls the day she stood helplessly watching as the museum was looted. In 2003, when the Americans entered Baghdad. She was very young at the time, she was with her fellow history students, and the pillage took place right before their eyes. There was nothing they could do. The Americans didn't lift a finger, they just let the thieves go in and out, smashing and stealing. Perhaps that is the day her vocation was born, in those hours of rage when she and her classmates watched the looters coming and going. Not her vocation as an archeologist, but as a hunter of lost objects. She thinks back now on all the hundreds of hours she has spent since that day searching for a trace of the stolen mosaics and statues and vases. Whenever an airport found an artifact in a collector's baggage, she was the one they called to come for the evaluation. A long struggle, twelve years already. But in a few days she will be rewarded: the National Museum is going to open its doors and the artifacts will once again be in their place.

Who fired the first shot? No one knows, but they all heard it. There. For kilometers. The first shot of what will turn out to be a mass slaughter. At five o'clock in the morning on this day when one country is going to kill another . . . Haile Selassie has given the order to attack and the Italians hurry to rouse themselves. Short phrases, rumors circulate: "It's started . . . They're attacking . . . " And in an hour, perhaps, the news will reach Marshal Badoglio himself. An aide-de-camp will wake him with the greatest possible dignity: "Marshal," he will say, looking straight ahead so that his gaze will not fall on the flaccid flesh protruding between the open buttons of the Marshal's pajamas, "Marshal, the battle has begun." The first shot and already thousands of men are running across the plain. Haile Selassie is toward the rear, standing straight in his European uniform. He will fight to the end. He will send reinforcements to Ras Kassa if necessary. But for now he has to wait, give the warriors time to run, to get closer to the enemy lines. The clamor reaches his ears. He wishes he could run with them, feel them all around him, share their sweat.

At Charles de Gaulle airport Assem Graieb thinks about his meeting with Auguste in Zurich, and the man from the American intelligence agency who was with them: Dan Kovac. He remembers how the discussion started. "We've got a problem with one of our men," said Kovac. Then he took out an envelope and showed them some photographs. Sullivan Sicoh. Forty-one years old. Former SEAL Team Six. One of McRogan's men. "This photo was taken two days before he left on a mission to northern Afghanistan. Things didn't go well there. He came back in smithereens . . . " explained Dan Kovac. Assem looked calmly at Sullivan Sicoh's face without speaking.

Sullivan enters the restaurant. He is one of the last ones and his friends shout for joy when they see him—the way they always do when one of them comes in. They hand him a glass and he drinks. In two days he'll be leaving for Kalafgan but he hasn't heard that name, yet, doesn't know that it will be the name of his wound. All he knows is that he's being sent to the Kunduz region in northern Afghanistan. Would he drink more if he knew that he will come close to losing his life? He listens to the jokes people make about him, answers back. He smiles, claps his palms together, gives hugs, takes a seat on the bench at the back and lets himself be submerged by the noise his friends are making, maybe they're celebrating nothing other than the fact that they're alive, and that's fine by him, so he drinks, too, as much as the others and then some. Later, when everyone is there, when they've squeezed together as best they can around this table initially meant for eight, and they number at least twelve, one of them asks the restaurant owner to take their picture, as if to have proof that at that moment they are all alive. Men between the ages of thirty and forty, well built, who know how to keep a cool head, men who have killed, who have known fear, who are able to immerse themselves in the silence of action, but who just now want to laugh and forget. He can feel them shoving, to his right, to his left, someone putting a hand on his shoulder—everyone has to fit in the photo. He smiles, or at least thinks he's smiling, but he doesn't realize that he's not.

Assem stares for a long time at the photograph. He has known so many men like this one: the impressive build, the face that is likeable even with an assault rifle in his hands. Of all the photographs, the one at the meal strikes him most: Sicoh is there amid all the others, all raising their glasses. It's easy to imagine the corny jokes, the slaps on the back, the tales of feats of arms told over and over. But Sicoh isn't smiling. He is staring at the camera lens with a strange depth to his gaze.

What isn't visible in the photograph is the divorce that has just been finalized. Nor is his final visit to the house where he lived for fifteen years, or how he left through the back door, distraught, exhausted, not even sure himself whether to be devastated or relieved. What isn't visible is the village of

Kalafgan, waiting for him, with mothers on their knees, his body battered and dragged through the dust, saved at the last minute by the arrival of the helicopter. What isn't visible in the photograph is the conviction that came over him during dinner, there amid his comrades' somewhat forced laughter, that he will not end up just one more divorced soldier, patiently waiting his turn to see his son, organizing barbecues on Sundays to try and transform the time with his son into something festive, then seeing in the boy's eyes that his barbecue is pathetic. What isn't visible in the photograph is what has vanished. His buddies all around him, shouting and singing. It is no longer possible to speak. It doesn't matter. He didn't go there to talk. And even when the rowdiest among them have calmed down, even when there is a time for quieter conversations, in little groups, as they hand each other cigarettes out on the sidewalk and enjoy a bit of fresh air, he won't say anything, won't talk to anyone about his divorce, not that he's ashamed or feels he has to hide anything, but because, already, he is no longer that man. Perhaps even then he senses that Kalafgan is waiting for him, and that this place will help him let his former self die.

At the airport Assem thinks of Dan Kovac's voice as he was showing him the photograph. He explained that Sullivan Sicoh has disappeared. He has given no sign of life to anyone. His ex-wife did not seem to be in any hurry to have news of him. The Americans knew he was in Beirut. At that point Kovac took out another photograph. "This is the only recent photograph we have of him, taken three months ago," he said. It showed a bearded man who didn't look anything like the guy from Michigan with the thick hands and broad smile. He looked, rather, like the guru of some sect, or a prisoner on the run. He was crossing a street. He had lost weight and let his hair and beard grow. His nervous eyes were looking anxiously across at the other sidewalk. Dan Kovac began talking. He seemed embarrassed. He explained that the situation for them had become rather awkward. That Sullivan Sicoh was dealing in all sorts of trafficked goods, with all sorts of people. Artifacts stolen from archeological sites. Weapons, too . . . He said they needed to find out what was his true state of mind. Assem remembers clearly the words he used. "What is his true state of mind . . . " And then Kovac added, "He's from an elite unit. He was at Abbottabad in 2011. He's a solid guy. And he knows an awful lot . . . " Silence fell again. Assem tried to imagine the man, how he had been during the famous raid that had led to bin Laden's death. He saw again the images of the raid on Abbottabad: helicopters attacking at night, the three shots fired at the Al-Qaeda leader, then the exfiltration . . . Auguste had to come out with his question, to ask explicitly what it was the Americans expected from their French counterparts, before Dan Kovac finally explained: "We'd be very grateful if you could get close to him and . . . assess him." Assem looked up abruptly, surprised. Assess him? That's not what he was used for, as a rule. The meeting was heading in a surprising direction; he asked why they hadn't contacted the Brits, instead. Looking him straight in the eye, Kovac replied that the French were better at handling the Beirut sector, and above all, Sicoh would be more wary of a Brit. And then he added that he left it up to his judgment. The basic aim was to determine whether Sicoh could still be "rehabilitated."

"And if he can't?" asked Auguste.

The American paused for a moment.

"Then we would be very grateful if you would arrange to have him neutralized."

Assem recalls that moment perfectly. The words are still echoing inside him. That is what awaits him. The people surrounding him in this terminal have no idea, but he is on the hunt. All around him there are families waiting for boarding to begin so they can get in line with their boarding passes in hand; there are businessmen typing hurriedly on their tablets. He has been sitting a little to one side in order to concentrate. He remembers perfectly the moment the man's death was first mentioned. And then, as if to justify himself, Kovac looked apologetic, and continued.

"Sullivan has been seen in a number of spots in the Middle East. If his trafficking is limited to art, we are ready to forget about it, but we have to be sure of his state of mind. No one in the Agency wants him to start writing his memoirs, if you see what I mean . . . "

Assem is about to board a plane for Beirut now, with the following mission: get close to a man who, from one day to the next, left everything behind; talk to him, get a good sense of who he is in order to determine whether he must be sentenced to death or can be rehabilitated. And there, in his seat at the airport, among all the men and women dragging their suitcases, each feeling a bit lonely in this suspended time, he wonders if they will do the same with him someday. He tries to imagine a contrite Auguste getting in touch with some friendly agency . . . Someday in a café, in Vienna or who knows where, will Auguste hand someone a photograph of him, Assem, and say, "We have a problem with Assem Graieb . . . ?"

"Have they seen the elephants?" Hannibal asks for the third time and the men around him hesitate: yes, they've seen them, it was impossible not to see them, but they don't know if their answer will unleash their leader's anger, or, on the contrary, make him smile. So they remain silent and look down. Then finally a Numidian horseman sits up very straight on his horse and says, "Yes, Hannibal, they saw them."

Hannibal gazes at the Rhône river behind him and the bodies scattered on the ground. The first of the Roman Empire's dead lie there, helmets pierced, hands still clinging to their swords or their wounds, faces distorted by pain or frozen in stupor. It is hot. The month of August weighs on the riverbanks and makes the mosquitoes dance. The first battle against the Romans has just been fought. A skirmish more than a battle, but from now on Rome can no longer ignore the fact that the Barcids are marching toward her. The news will spread. The soldiers who retreated will tell what they saw. They will talk about the army made up of Iberians, Gauls, and Numidians. They will be questioned about the exact number of men in the enemy's army, about the proportion of horsemen and foot soldiers. And above all, they will talk about the elephants . . . Hannibal smiles. The forty elephants he has brought with him will grow, will become enormous, bloodthirsty monsters. The stories will take form. There will no longer be forty elephants, but eighty, a hundred . . . And fear will spread all around. Yes, they have seen the elephants. And every passing day, from now on, will sap the Romans' morale. They will be more and more afraid. Time will wear them down, the time this long march takes. The Alps are still far away. There may be other clashes, but Hannibal is in no hurry. He has to let the rumors precede him. Already, wherever he goes, people have let him through, they do not dare oppose his army, the likes of which they've never seen. Why should they? To be loyal to Rome? No. They have seen with Saguntum where loyalty to Rome can get you. So they have let Hannibal pass through their villages, their territory, they even fed them now and again and, when they saw the long column of forty elephants laden with parcels, weapons, and shields, they prayed to their gods that they would never have to fight any creatures like that. And they wondered: if these creatures were indeed as formidable as they seemed, would they see the fall of Rome in their lifetimes?

"Colonel?" A voice calling, somewhat timorous. He hears but cannot reply. His body won't obey him. "Colonel?" He tries to hold out his hand to prop himself on the table, but it seems as if this hand is making a fool of him, and he slumps over. What did he expect? That all he had to do was leave Illinois and his father's tannery, which is what he did, not even ten days after the fall of Fort Sumter, for a new life to begin? That all he had to do was put on his uniform, to be cleansed of his former self? That acting as a recruiter, which is what he has been doing for weeks, would eliminate the shame, banish his demons?

He keeps his eyes closed. The world around him is plunged in darkness. All that's left is that voice. "Colonel . . . ?" He is dead drunk. Can't they tell? The young man who just came through the door should stop being so solicitous, should go and get a bowl of water and splash it in his face, or else leave him where he is to sleep off his sadness, but just leave him alone! Yes he's been drinking. Two whole bottles. Worth every drop. He has just heard that the Union army got trounced at Bull Run. And yet there were so many of them. General McDowell is useless. And Beauregard must have smiled again, the way he smiled at Fort Sumter. Bunch of imbeciles . . . They went to war the way you go to a parade. The Confederates have not made the same mistake. They know they can't afford the luxury. Thomas Jackson's Virginians came to fight, and they held their ground. That's how the Yankees should have gone about it, with the deep conviction that defeat is out of the question. The land of the founding fathers cannot be divided. The shame will be theirs if they let the secession go through. The shame will be theirs if slavery is allowed to prosper. McDowell is useless. He wants to win his fine battles but that's not what war is about. You have to win, period. Which means crushing the war itself, and that can only be done through violence. The Virginians have just taught them a lesson. They held on, with a rage to win. They stood their ground, until Beauregard ordered the counterattack and the Union ranks were routed. Apparently the ladies in Washington, sure of their victory, had come out in their fine carriages to watch the show, with cold chicken and refreshments. They must have wet themselves, stupid hens, cursing their own curiosity, when to everyone's amazement Stonewall Jackson charged with his troops, mowing down everything in his way and driving the Yankees back. He ought to admire the Confederates' determination. He ought to be glad of McDowell's collapse, but there were youngsters who had died, and what was trampled on the battlefield was the abolition of slavery and the direction of History. A curse upon those men who don't take war seriously. Yes, he's been drinking. Because he has been thinking about them, all those young men who died in the space of just a few minutes, and for nothing, incredulous as they discovered that bullets really do whistle and will shatter their skulls on impact. "Colonel?" He hears the young man's voice again and he wants to yell at him to get out, scram, leave him alone with his disgrace and his drunken self . . . He thought it would be enough to inform his wife that he was going to enlist for everything to go back to normal, but he still wants to drink, even if he can't even stand up, he wants to drink because the Union forces have been routed, they've retreated in scattered companies, stunned, filthy with mud, leaving Sherman's cannons behind with the cold chicken thighs, the picnic tablecloths, the Confederate cries of victory.

On the Maychew plain the Italians are awake. In response to the first shots, the first shells fall and Haile Selassie's first soldiers die. The Italians have no reason to panic. They have built a wall of dried earth to protect their line, and they have allowed the Ethiopians to get closer. The day is slowly dawning. The plain will soon be covered in blood. The shells are falling steadily. This is how they will kill them, by scattering them, smashing them, blowing them to smithereens. The Ethiopian warriors' triumphant victory at Adwa will not be seen again. Italy wants her revenge. That is precisely why she has come. And she will get it. What will Haile Selassie's place be in History? That of a defeated emperor? The king of kings killed by the explosion of a shell? The battle is under way, and from now on the entire day will be devoted to slaughter. Advance. Shout to muster courage and moan when the bullet goes through you. Oh, what a long time a defeat takes . . . You have to live through it completely, right to the end, live through those moments when you still believe there's a chance, and the calls for help you cannot answer, friends dying, then those magnificent breaches—and sometimes the sun, the beauty of your surroundings . . . It's taking so long . . . The smell of blood and gunpowder is everywhere. And then, the day slowly starts to fade, after thirteen hours of battle where the Ethiopians, some of them bare-chested, have been charging at heavy machine guns. Seventy-five tons of explosives relentlessly blowing them to bits. Italy doesn't matter. The Duce was categorical: he wants a brilliant victory, and a quick one. After thirteen hours of fighting he's got it. And the Negus orders the withdrawal. But that is when the unthinkable happens. Because the defeat is hungry for more. The Italians leave their line and go after the enemy. Haile Selassie sees the brutal wave surging behind his men. Planes fly over the battlefield, strafing the fugitives. Gas burns those who try to run. Everything explodes, twists. It is no longer a withdrawal, it is a debacle, a massacre. They are annihilated. And on it goes. "There's nothing we can do," he thinks. He has offered his men up to this carnage. And then finally, with the sudden onset of night, the sky itself begins to thunder. A storm breaks, violent, terrifying. Lightning streaks the sky and whenever it does it reveals a host of moaning. The dying are there on the ground, on the battlefield, in the mud, stiff and cold or still moaning, their mouths open, they are astonished by this air that is killing them, they do not understand how this can be, and a hard rain falls, as if it were trying to drown everything. Perhaps the very sky is disgusted by what it has seen. Men go back for their dead but cannot find them; they grope about among an ocean of corpses. It's all over. And the dying open their eyes wide to hear the roar of thunder one last time, to feel a little of the cool rain on lips that soon will be cold.

He can hear teeth chattering all around him. The men are cold. Should he give up? No. He has to go on to the end. He clenches his jaw. His entire body is growing stiff on his horse. He is trembling in spite of the animal hides on his shoulders. Some of his best Numidian horsemen, feverish, their eyes yellow, their lips white, he can see them still clinging on but they are unsteady, and eventually they will fall and no one will be able to help them. They will die the way so many others have, there by the side of these stony paths, amid the first snows, they will be astonished to have it end like this, on the cold earth, so far away from home, without even having fought a battle. His army is melting in the snow. For ten days already they have been advancing, ruining their horses' hooves, leaving the sick elephants behind, forcing their way through the mist on the summits. The local populace watch them go by and they spit on the ground or throw stones at them before skittering away down invisible trails. Should he give up and turn back? Can he return to Carthage and hand the power over to Hannon, the old family enemy who is just waiting for one mistake, one sign of weakness to take things in hand and seal a pact with the Romans? All around him men are dying. The biting cold allows them no respite. Every morning they tally the number of those who died in the night, every morning there are animals—horses, mules, elephants—that refuse to get up and the men have to remove their bundles and salvage what they can. He has heard the death rattle of men on horseback, seen them die as they sit in their saddles, as if frozen, until their mounts fall into the ravine. He has seen the elephants go mad from the pain and charge the men who have imposed this torture upon them, trampling those who might have survived, taking everything with them, their rage, their drivers, the clusters of dumbstruck soldiers. Half of the elephants have died. There are only twenty left. According to Mago, they will lose fifteen thousand men before they reach the other side of the Alps. And Rome must be smiling to see the mountains wearing her enemies down like this, starving them, making them shiver. Rome must be smiling, because the cold is destroying them. It has even begun to affect Hannibal himself. For the last few days he has only been able to see out of one eye. It got infected and he knows that if a fever takes hold he will be done for. It often seems to him that his horse is walking too close to the edge, that it will fall, but that is because he cannot see. He keeps going in spite of everything. If the mountains are to be his tomb, let them take him as he is, on horseback, his gaze toward Rome. Perhaps he is mad to have wanted to come this way. He is mad to have sentenced more than fifteen thousand of his men to death, to have thought they would find passes through this unfamiliar land, that the elephants would survive the cold wind from the glaciers. He is mad but so much the better, because it is madness that will be the cornerstone of his legend. And never mind if he has to sacrifice an eye to the mountains, never mind if half of his army melts away: if they make it over, well, then they will be truly terrifying.

The thousands of possibilities, coincidences, crossroads, improbabilities that life offers, incessantly. And maybe, in short, that is all life ever is: negotiating a passage through the vagaries. She thinks about the man, Assem Graieb. Their paths crossed one night and they will probably never meet again.

They have gone back to their own lives, their own random fates. She has rediscovered who she is: how she spends her time, her office, the trip to Baghdad for the museum opening, her illness as well. She is back in that story, and suddenly it seems heavy, boring, as if what Assem had given her that night, above and beyond the physical pleasure, above and beyond the smiles, the charm, was a kind of self-forgetfulness. For a whole night, she was no one. Just a name, a smile, a body. She had a respite from herself. And now she has to return to that self. She is busy picking up her files but then just as she is about to leave the UNESCO building her colleague Krystin comes into her office, her face white.

"Mariam, have you seen the news?"

She doesn't answer, presses her lips, can already sense that what Krystin is about to tell her will hurt.

"You have to see this . . . They've taken Mosul . . . "

It is like a slap in the face. At first she cannot believe it. Then her colleague leads her to a television and on the news channel they watch the images, stunned. Columns of pickup trucks moving along the roads of northern Iraq, long black flags fluttering from the rear. Men who have sworn allegiance to death, now hamming it up for the cameras. It is the start of something. It is as if these men are marching on her. They will not leave her unharmed, they have arisen out of the depths of obscurity, their weapons in hand, to destroy what she has been patiently building for years. She senses that everything she believes in is in danger, confronted now with these men. And she thinks at once of the artifacts in the museum, in Mosul.

He takes his seat in the plane. By the window, toward the front. Next to him a Lebanese couple are speaking a mixture of Arabic and English. He looks out the window. All along the runway, wind socks are beginning to dance. The wind is rising, as if it had come out of nowhere. "Are you ready to go?" asks his uncle again in a corner of his mind. He thinks of Mycenae, the town spilling down onto the plain of Argos, all those men who do not understand that they have already lost, that they will never stop bleeding from their war. And Assem, what will he lose in Beirut? What will he forfeit to the wind by accepting this mission? A man is waiting there, whom he may have to kill. This is not what frightens him the most. What he dreads is having to speak to him, listen to him, engage with him in order to assess the situation. Until now, whenever he was assigned a mission he had a target. He had to find the prey, and kill him. But in this case, he will have to decide. What, with this man, will he weigh in the balance to determine whether he should die or not? Is dealing with stolen art reason enough? Assem mulls it all over, and the wind is blowing harder and harder. Clouds are hurrying ever more quickly across the sky. The sound of the wind is audible in the aircraft. The plane is moving, taxiing toward the runway. "Are you ready to go?" He is ready. He gives his consent to be amputated. Every departure is a loss. That is what he wanted to tell his uncle, and perhaps he was right. He thinks again of the meeting in Zurich. Before leaving, Dan Kovac added that Sicoh had surrounded himself with an odd little band, a strange bunch, neither really political nor religious . . . A Cuban, a Syrian, a woman from Colombia, some Palestinians, two Libyans, some Egyptians as well, and Sicoh reigns over them like a warlord. He also told him that the American calls himself Job. What are they so afraid of? This unlikely group? Or something Sullivan Sicoh has seen . . . He was at the prison at Abu Ghraib in 2004. He was part of McRogan's inner team. Maybe McRogan has political ambition and is worried about what his men might say about him . . . Or maybe Dan Kovac didn't tell him everything about Sicoh's friends in Beirut. Maybe some are agents from other countries? It could be any number of things. Sullivan Sicoh. He thinks about the man he is on his way to find, and who doesn't know him yet. A man with a bushy beard and fine braids in his long hair. Does he know that the United States is worried about him, about what he says, what he sells? Does he know that they're sending someone to try and suss him out? Yes. He's bound to know. That is even, surely, why he chose Beirut, to frighten the people he left behind. Sullivan Sicoh. The more he thinks about him, the more he seems to know him. They are two of a kind. They were trained in the same school, in the same battle. They have obeyed the same orders, run the same risks, been frightened by the same ordeals. Both of them have seen what man can do to man: the very worst. Sullivan Sicoh. Yes, he knows him. The wind blows, lifts the plane: it takes off in a growl of engines. In only a few seconds Paris is behind him. He is between earth and sky, his sole companion that man who is still only a name; but he is eager to meet him.

III
ERBIL

She wept when she saw the images of the museum in Mosul, shown over and over on the news channels: a man wearing a dishdasha, an angle grinder in his hand, hard at work on the great winged colossus. Others smashing a statue with a mallet. She put her hand over her mouth, as if she were about to cry out, or throw up. Yet she knows how violent these men are, looting, raping, killing. She knows her country is falling apart while this army advances, their black flag brandishing the name of Allah, and that they are just one more aspect of the obscurantism that has always existed, that likes neither music, nor women, nor knowledge, nor the freedom of peoples. She knows all that. There are reports of huge columns of refugees fleeing the north, trying to reach Iraqi Kurdistan. It is said that the Yazidis are trapped in the Sinjar mountains, starving, and they are shown no mercy—women, children, old people. Is that not worse, their blood, those mothers searching in vain for a refuge, those faces gaunt with fatigue, still fleeing, always fleeing, endlessly? Is that not worse than a few nicks of the angle grinder against stone? When Mosul fell, she followed the news by the hour, saddened and dismayed, but she didn't cry. Whereas every gash this man makes to the face of the stone giant with the braided beard makes her sick. The images on the news show the chaos in the museum. Objects overturned, display windows smashed. Artifacts are grabbed and stuffed in pockets. Others are thrown to the floor with a cry of "Allahu Akbar"; smashed for eternity, the sadness of the few seconds that suffice to annihilate vases and statues that had survived for centuries. Those men overturning urns and striking statues: they think they are subjugating time itself. Oh, it took so long for those artifacts to reach us. The men and women who devoted their life to the cause: Paul-Émile Botta, the consul of Mosul who discovered Khorsabad and brought back the great bulls that have pride of place in the Mesopotamian rooms at the Louvre. Gertrude Bell, who took part in the creation of Iraq at the summit in Cairo, where she had Churchill's ear and where Lawrence of Arabia nodded, concurring with her analyses; she also wanted to leave the country she loved with a museum, and founded what would become the Baghdad Antiquities Museum, later the National Museum of Iraq. Hormuzd Rassam, the little boy from Mosul who was sixteen when Botta came to his town, and who ended up in Brighton, but not before discovering the oldest manuscript of *Gilgamesh* . . . All those men who dug and thought and searched and failed and searched again. All those anonymous hands, helping with a pickaxe, raising dust and sand, caressing a newly-found object before passing it on to the excavation leader. All those artifacts patiently dusted, weighed, examined: the centuries had looked after them and now they have ended up here, hurled against the wall, "Allahu Akbar": how can they even say those words, when all they express is the ugliness and intoxication of destruction?

The first days after his return from Afghanistan—or the first hours—he is incapable of saying how much time had gone by—the room in the military hospital seemed enormous to Sullivan Sicoh, and he did not even try to encompass it with his gaze. He felt it was beyond his strength. He saw bodies, sensed presences, the medical staff coming and going by his bedside, to change a bandage, a drip, his own silent thick drip or that of other patients in beds nearby, who occasionally made a

sound—a moan, a call, a murmur to themselves—a sign that
there was still life in them, however faint, however much that
life moaned, a life thoroughly shattered. And then gradually
the spells of consciousness grew longer, and now he can open
his eyes more decisively. They sit him up in bed and he can see
all of the room, smaller than he'd pictured it. Broken bodies.
Emaciated men with pale complexions, restless or drowsy.
Here he is, back from Kalafgan and in this strangely calm ward
of suffering (you'd think that all these young men in here—all
valiant soldiers only a few weeks ago—would be screaming,
protesting, demanding that the vigor and wholeness of their
bodies be restored to them), the nurses wander around like
nuns in a convent, hardly moving the air, just the faint light
sound of their steps to signal their presence. He looks around
him at the broken bodies, the faces full of pain, and he decides
that this ward, these beds are not a place of rest and recon-
struction, but a place he must run from as soon as he can, that
these patients around him are not brothers, but shadows from
whom he must flee.

Hannibal touches his eye with his fingertip. There is no
more pus. Has it healed? Has his body triumphed over the
gangrene? The wound is no longer oozing. He looks out at the
horizon, swaying to the slow pace of his horse. He cannot see
anything, never again will he see anything, with that eye. But
it doesn't matter. The swamps of the Arno have taken an eye
from him. So be it. This Roman empire, on whose ground he
is now walking, this empire he has been fighting since his
arrival, has had its opportunity to mark his flesh. It's only fair.
It is total war that lies ahead and perhaps he will lose even
more, perhaps one eye is only the beginning. All through the
campaigns to come, his body will pay the price. He must
accept this possibility. So many of his own people will be
wounded. So many will follow him, despite lameness or an

atrophied hand. The farther they go, the greater the number of crippled men among them. It is only fair that he should know what it means to be on the same footing as his men. War is raging. He is facing Publius Cornelius Scipio. One of them must give way, and it will be the Roman. He has already begun to falter: during the battle at Ticinus, then at Trebbia. He very nearly died on the battlefield, during their first confrontation. The Romans panicked, were terrified, no longer knew what to do. Custom held that in the art of war a winter truce must be honored, but Hannibal ordered his men to continue advancing, despite the cold. They marched on Rome in November, in December, and sometimes there was snow. The elephants died one after the other but nothing could stop the army's indomitable advance. During the battle at Trebbia, they covered their bodies in oil to protect against the cold, and it was the Romans who died, numbed, too slow, their teeth chattering when it came time to fight, their bodies shivering when they should have been taking aim. Hannibal would lose an eye, yes, but he was advancing. And the Senate was beginning to quake in its boots. Cornelius Scipio seems not to know how to wage a battle anymore, whereas the arms of the Numidian rebels do not tremble. So, surely Hannibal can sacrifice an eye to the Roman soil. What did they all think? That they could ride to victory and remain immaculate? That from so much fighting they could emerge unharmed, fresh as daisies? Since crossing Gibraltar he has given his life over to war. This means his body, his time, his thoughts. There will be injuries, and cries. There will be scars and terror, and if that is all, then he can consider himself lucky. The Romans have not understood this, and they are slowly realizing that what is about to happen will be neither clean nor respectful. There will be no panache. Everything is dirty and terrifying, just like the corpses of the Romans drowned in the snow-swollen waters of the Trebbia—those men with blue lips, bodies stiff with cold, floating drearily. He has lost an eye, it is true. He will go around half-blind now, but this matters little to him, so long as they keep advancing.

"For the moment, they like me," he thinks, there in his tent, while an aide-de-camp brings a letter informing him that General Buell is stalled and therefore they will confront Johnston's army on their own. "They like me because I was victorious at Fort Henry and Fort Donaldson, and I'm one of the only senior officers from the Union to have a few victories to my name . . . " He thinks of McClellan, who is indecisive, McClellan who always waits for months as if he were afraid to move his pawns across the Geological Survey map. Because the men are pawns. There is no other way to look at it. Or then you shouldn't be a general. There are no farmers, no kindly fathers, no overgrown schoolboys with jolly faces and wide-spaced teeth, there are no husbands, there are only units. Otherwise, how could you decide to send this battalion to the front and not that one? How could you order a group to go on a diversionary mission when you know there is a good chance they won't make it back? Only Sherman understands this. Because he's crazy, and he knows that the men don't count anymore, that you have to accept this way of thinking and that in so doing you forfeit your right to call yourself human. And because he knows all that, he is crazy. And besides, Sherman is brave. Not brave in the ordinary sense of the word, which is merely a variation on obedience. How many men perform heroic acts simply because they have been ordered to, because they don't have the strength to say no? With Sherman it is something else. He is courageous because he refuses to accept defeat. It consumes him. Defeat makes him want to bite someone, to spur the sides of his horse and charge all alone into the enemy ranks. He disobeys the normal course of events. And not many men have this gift. That is why he was the only one who fought at Bull Run, the only one who truly refused to be in on the spoils. Yes, Sherman can understand. All the others will turn their backs on him when the men begin to fall. "For the time being, they like me," he thinks, "but that will change." He curses. The aide-de-camp thinks it's because of the news he has just brought, but he is mistaken. It is not the fact Buell is delayed that worries him. He is furious because he fell off his horse yesterday and that means that today he has to use crutches to get up out of his camp bed. He is furious because this injury will prevent him from riding into the thick of the battle, when that is where the course of fate will be determined. He knows that things will get ugly, and in a vague sort of way he can sense it will be soon. The only difference between him and his men and the Confederates, is their cause. It's not nothing. They have to cling to that. The rest is going to be ugly. The men will start killing each other on a grand scale, and they have to resist. The soldiers, whatever side they are on, will be immersed in the fire and the fray, and it is with astonishment that they will discover the sordid face of murder.

Sullivan Sicoh looks all around at the bodies that have been there with him for months, and what he sees is war and debacle. In the wounds, the disabilities, the stumps, the lowered gazes, the tears of helplessness. Like everyone else, he focuses hard to perform his reeducation exercises. He has to build up his muscles again, his body having melted away from the long days lying in bed, he has to unravel the tension that at times makes him look like an old man. He has to fill out, force his muscles to regain their elasticity. He tries to focus in order to forget all the rest, including the pain. Inch by inch, day by day, he reconquers some territory of his own life. He wants to become who he once was and, slowly, he is getting there. He can tell he is making progress. The physiotherapists have told him so. He is recovering his vitality. And then one morning the doctor comes to see him and he knows from the smile on his face that today they won't be doing any exercises, that they've finished, he has reclaimed the use of his body. So he lets the doctor come up to him and before he has time to say a single word, Sullivan looks at him and says, "Are we done? Am I good to go out and kill again?"

In her office at UNESCO she wept. The images were all the same, and the disgust was always new. Until she remembered how greedy men can be. Islamic State, like others before them, will listen to money. They already know that what they are doing terrifies the world and that it is possible to earn vast sums of money with these artifacts that are lying on the floor. The angle grinder was merely to raise the stakes. Behind it lies the door to a vast traffic in stolen art. So she knows she must go there. And that is also what the head of cultural heritage tells her when she enters her office, pale, holding a folder in her hand that she hasn't been able to read because all morning all she could do, dumbfounded, was watch the images playing over and over on the television. "If there is anyone who should be there right now, it's you. Never mind the inauguration at the Baghdad museum. You'll be more useful in Mosul. There might be a few items you can still save . . . " Mariam knows she's right, and that she has to act quickly. So without hesitating she throws a few belongings in a bag and boards a flight for Erbil.

"They're attacking!" Grant sits up in his bunk and looks at his watch. It is six A.M. He hears the first shots. How can they already be so close? He gets up, grimaces when his foot touches the floor—he'd forgotten about his fall—and hurries to put on his tunic. "They're attacking!" Sherman leaps up, too, and Prentiss and Wallace, all the Union officers who are camping with their men around the little church at Shiloh. How many are they? Where are they? They are all getting up.

The enlisted men reach for their rifles. The officers saddle their horses. The artillerymen get busy and already the enemy is upon them. The Confederates arrive in a thick wave. They are running, shouting to give themselves courage, glad of the element of surprise they have created, the panic they can see in the Yankee ranks. They have to form a line of defense as quickly as possible. Not scatter. Not give way to fear. Regroup. And hold fast. At any cost. Hold fast. Grant says it, then repeats it. Otherwise, they will be blown to pieces . . .

"Sack the villages!" From the top of the hill where he has pitched his camp Hannibal looks down at the graceful slopes of Tuscany in the gentle late-afternoon light. Everything here is beautiful: the vineyards on the hillsides, the cypress trees dotting the fields. Everything is opulent and peaceful. His men hesitate, look at him. Are those really his orders? He can see they do not believe him so he repeats it, "Tell your men to destroy everything." He knows what this means. He knows how rough the Balearic rebels will be when they break down doors and throw themselves upon everything—women, animals, wine—to satisfy a monstrous appetite, to forget the hardship of the Alps and the scorching sun upon the glaciers. He knows it will get ugly, that their robes will be torn in the mud, that houses will be set ablaze and villages razed to the ground. But this is the region of Flaminius, the commander of the Roman legions, and he must be defied, needled, made to lose his composure. Some men go to war on the condition that it will not touch them. They agree to put their own lives in the balance, yes, but not their wives' or their children's, or their cellars full of amphorae of oil and local wine, or the beautiful houses they have inherited. Flaminius is one of those men. Hannibal can tell. He will lay waste to the entire region, and the Roman will lose his clear-sightedness and his composure.

Everything is a question of composure, and Sherman has no lack of it. He gathers his men and reforms his line of defense. Prentiss, in the center, does likewise. They must stand firm. The Confederates are upon them. The first wave knocks them over like a sword thrust in the belly. The dead men fall, only just roused from sleep, their faces now forever frozen in the morning chill. "Take me to the battlefield!" orders Grant. He wants to get as close as possible. He knows that it is composure that will make the difference, and he has plenty. In this respect he and Sherman are twins. They remain equally calm in the fray, they have the same ability to read troop movements in the crush. He speaks to his men, berates them, encourages them. He wants to know who is overwhelmed and who is resisting, where reinforcements are needed . . . That is how battles are won, by controlling the fear that is constantly trying to make you turn tail and thrusts you toward death just when you thought you were saved.

Her plane has just left Vienna. She is headed east. Soon she will fly over Turkey and then northern Iraq. Soon she will pass above Mosul, the gutted museum, the barbarians gleeful of their misdeeds, these layers of History that are her life, there below, in this region that is constantly set ablaze.

The waves follow, one after the other. Who can withstand such an onslaught of power? Eight, ten, twelve, more than fifteen attacks are launched against the Yankee line of defense. The Confederates are indefatigable. They charge again and again . . . Bodies mingle, in an embrace of death. The enemy is no longer visible, so dense is the cloud of gunpowder and smoke. Hold fast. Grant keeps saying the words, like a prayer. And that is what Prentiss and his men do, at the forward post, for over seven consecutive hours. They hold fast, to give Grant and the others time to get organized, to give Buell time to arrive and take up his position. Then at last they surrender. Aching, stunned, their faces splattered with the blood of those who fell by their side, enemies or brothers, they surrender, and General Johnston smiles. He has not yet understood that this surrender is not a victory for him; Prentiss may be capitulating but Sherman has had time to take up a new position, as has Wallace. Grant is more determined than ever. The wind has changed. And only Johnston fails to understand that as Prentiss advances, battered by all the blows given and received, looking gaunt and exhausted, his uniform in tatters, it is as a victor. Because from now on the battle will start to go the other way.

She flies over the war-torn land between Mosul and Erbil. That is where Alexander beat Darius. That is where Paul-Émile Botta found and excavated Dur-Sharrukin. These lands have never stopped bleeding, for centuries empires have clashed and their people have fled from war. Her own life consists of digging, unearthing, preserving. What is the point, if the world is on fire? Should she not, rather, take up a gun to try and check the killers' advance? So many questions reeling through her. Of course she shouldn't. It's absurd. She knows very well that she is fighting, in her way, but she cannot help but think again of the man with the angle grinder. And what if he were standing there before her, would she be prepared to kill him to protect the great colossus?

Not a sound. The thick fog seems to be stifling everything. The birds have fallen silent. The Romans cannot even hear the sound of their own footsteps on the ground. Everything is silence. They advance. Flaminius wants to have done with Hannibal. So that never again will any barbarian be in a position to burn the villages of Tuscany. So that never again will Rome experience the humiliation of trembling before the enemy.

The Carthaginians try not to breathe, not to let their weapons rattle. They wait. It is now that the outcome will be decided. And they know it. Lake Trasimene is not far from here; they have taken up their positions high on the hills above the valley. If the Romans pass below them, in the narrow defile along the river, they will have won. If the sky clears and they become visible, all will be lost. Hannibal waits. He knows that the day's outcome no longer depends on him. A sound, a horse whinnying, a cloud shifting—anything can change the course of History. And then suddenly one of his men goes up to him and murmurs in a thick voice, "They have entered the defile." So he stands and orders his men to hurl themselves upon the enemy.

"Charge!"
General Johnston himself is participating in the attack, and he plants his spurs in his horse's sides. He thinks that all they have to do is finish the attack and it will all be over soon. The Yankees have withdrawn to Pittsburg Landing. He sees nothing to prevent him from making the most of his advantage. He thinks it is time to harry the defeated. "Charge!"

The Carthaginians scurry down the slope. And initially the Romans do not understand where the shouts are coming from, because the fog distorts sounds, displaces them. Until suddenly they see the men there, already upon them, careening down the hill to their left. The horses are frightened and rear up. The foot soldiers withdraw spontaneously toward the lake to avoid the attack. There is confusion everywhere, and no one can see a thing.

A bullet pierces Johnston's leg, near the top of his boot. The blood flows, sticky, thick. He thinks it is nothing serious, and stays on his horse. He does not know that the blood will continue to fill his boot and that in less than an hour he will be dead, there, at Shiloh, in this land that should have been a site of victory but which will, instead, be his grave.

The panic spreads everywhere. No one can control the men. Flaminius knows that if they lose their calm they will be lost. He shouts orders but no one can hear them in the fog. Everything goes to pieces. The Gauls are terrifying, with their braids and long beards. Then a horseman rushes at the consul and kills him with one blow. A little voice falls silent in the mêlée and the vast Roman army, without its leader, scatters in all directions.

"Charge!" Now it is Grant who is shouting. And Buell with him. Sherman, Wallace, and all the Yankee officers. It is their turn to advance. War is nothing else: this backwards and forwards, gaining territory or losing it. Standing one's ground or retreating. And having the strength to get back up, even after seven hours of combat, even after a night on the lookout, to attack the same enemy who tore you to pieces the day before. Beauregard, who has replaced Johnston, sees the Union troops counterattacking. He realizes it is all over. More men will die, but the battle of Shiloh has been lost and there is nothing for it but to retreat.

She glides over her gilded lands. Seen from here, everything looks calm. And yet she knows that on the ground there is war. People shooting, running, shouting. Villages will be shelled, positions taken and retaken. But from up here everything looks beautiful, vast and calm. She thinks of the Jesuit priest Antoine Poidebard, the inventor of aerial archeology. In the 1930s he crisscrossed the skies over Mesopotamia, flying over Beirut, Damascus, the Syrian desert, Palmyra . . . Hundreds of hours of flying time, his eyes riveted to the ground to locate buried Roman structures, the lines of walls that time had leveled, the traces of ancient fortifications. And the Bedouin tribes watched, stunned, as the plane flew overhead; sometimes they fired at it, for fear it might bring some misfortune. She thinks about Poidebard and how he too glided over the crush of countless lives beneath him. He saw the Roman *limes* in the Syrian desert. He could see Antiquity surfacing, because from his airplane it was so clear, you could not miss it, whereas down below the humans who walked along those roads or lived in those villages could not see it. She thinks of Antoine Poidebard and the amassing of time. It is all there beneath her: Alexander's campaigns, the wall that kept the Pax Romana, the lines that Churchill and the French drew during the Cairo Conference, the advance of Islamic State. She is gliding over time, over humans, their tiny destiny, and she doesn't even see them. From where she is, the only thing that is visible is the gilded land of the East.

For the victory to be real, it's not enough for the enemy be caught in a trap, with no way out and their leader dead; it's not enough for there to be no more orders to muster the troops, with each soldier thinking only of his own life, trying to flee, and trembling with fear. For the victory to be real, you have to go all the way, and once the enemy is driven back, with the lake behind them, at a loss what to do, then you must advance and kill them. That is what they are doing now. The Iberians, the Balearics, the Punic soldiers. They surround the Romans and slay them. They slice, stab, hack. They slaughter the men as if they were a herd of sheep. One by one, patiently. Fifteen thousand men. With the weariness of repeated gestures. They do it because only afterward will they truly be able to speak of victory, only later will the news reach Rome and, for the first time, panic will spread through the streets. They mutilate bodies and slit throats, one by one, until those fifteen thousand bodies stain the waters of the lake with their blood, fifteen thousand bodies of men who this morning thought they would live and now, three hours later, are floating while the fog lifts at last to offer Hannibal the gruesome spectacle of his victory. Perhaps he is gripped by that moment? Perhaps for those three hours of hand-to-hand combat they were brothers, united in having, all of them, placed their lives in the hands of fate? Perhaps that is why he searches for Flaminius's body on the battlefield for a long time, but he does not find it, because the consul was decapitated and his head rolled into the water; and so, Hannibal asks that they pay tribute to all the dead, including those whose throats his soldiers were still slitting only a few minutes earlier. And at last everyone falls silent as they stare at the red waters of the lake.

Grant knows that today he has won. He strides through the orchard at Shiloh, littered with bodies; he steps over the stiffened arms of the dead men. Around him, all the officers are dismayed by the extent of the loss. What did they think? Warfare is slaughter, that's all it is. Nothing else. Everyone is looking at him with disgust but he knows that he has won. Even if there is a surge of anger going all the way to Lincoln, even if from now on they will call him "the Butcher." Even if for a time they will remove him from positions of command because the other generals still dream of clean victories. He, Grant, knows the odor of battlefields. Once the smell of gunpowder has dissipated, the smell that is left is that of guts and blood. So why not, let them call him "the Butcher," basically they're right. So many men fell today. But he refuses to let anyone say that he lost, at Shiloh. It's a victory. This is what victories look like: the wounded men limp, and the dying ones moan, just as they do in defeat. The only thing that matters is that Beauregard is retreating and he, Ulysses S. Grant, is advancing. And so what if it's hell. Since it is a war, it has to be won.

The plane speeds across the skies of Turkey and Iraq and she seems to sense all those hundreds of millions of lives that ended in mutual massacre in these lands over the centuries. How much of all that is left? Statues, vases, temples, fortresses, staring at us in silence. Every era has known upheaval. What is left is what she, personally, is looking for. Not lives, anymore, individual destinies, but what humans have given to time, that part they want to rescue from the catastrophe, that part on which defeat has no hold, the gesture toward eternity. And today it is that part which the men in black are threatening. They wave their weapons and scream that they are not afraid of death. *"Viva la muerte!"* said the Spanish fascists. It is the same sort of arrogant pride, the same hatred of humankind. But what they are attacking, those men in black, is that which, normally, is exempt from battle and fire. They shoot and shell and burn the way men have always done. Antiquity is full of cities that have been ransacked—Persepolis burned, Tyre destroyed—but as a rule traces have always remained, as a rule man did not completely obliterate his enemy. What is happening now, with these men vomiting their hatred, is the ecstasy that comes with the power to erase History.

IV
BEIRUT

The Beirut heat gripped him the moment he left the airport, thick, briny air, carrying the commotion of traffic jams and the cries of children from the neighborhoods to the south. During the taxi ride to the hotel he gazed out at the streets, avidly, observing the changes in a city he has known for fifteen years: the buildings that have eventually collapsed from exhaustion, the new ones that have grown like huge glass flowers, with fountains and marble. Everything is adjacent here, ruins and real estate speculation, traces of the past (a bullet-riddled building, an old house in Achrafieh from the days of the French protectorate) and a desire to forget. They are all here, Christians and Muslims, faces of poverty and cosmopolitan smiles. He loves this city more than any other, with its dense violence, as old as a mountain vendetta; the nervous tension of the streets in Hamra and the majestic morning calm of the restaurants along the Corniche, where you can eat breakfast overlooking the sea. He loves this city that constantly hesitates between razing everything to the ground and rebuilding, or keeping it all so that the wounds of the past will be visible and serve as a lesson to the generations to come, hesitating and never deciding, because before it even has time to decide it is overcome yet again by its demons, voraciously self-harming, bleeding, tearing itself to shreds. He loves this city because the entire world is here—Druze, Kurds, Palestinians, Armenians, those who come back once a year to see their old mother, arriving from Cairo or Bamako, Beijing or Port-au-Prince, and who speak multiple languages because for years now the world has belonged to the Lebanese; they may tear their own country apart but they sail all the seas, these sons of Phoenicians. These days the city is splitting at the seams with the influx of refugees, a constant flow of Syrians. They look at the Palestinian camps that have turned into concrete cities, horrible places crammed together in an inextricable tangle of electric wires, and the Syrians know that is the best they can hope for: to stay here and get old as exiles in a city that has no tears left for those who flee their country, because the city itself still needs to fight to survive, still yearns for a dazed oblivion.

The plane landed and initially, at the airport, everything seemed normal. Then a car came to take her to the French Institute and they drove through town. Erbil is in a state of utter confusion. There are refugees converging from all sides, fleeing the advance of Islamic State. A few months ago the Iraqi Kurds took in their Syrian brothers. Refugee camps were built all along the northern border. In Domiz. In Kawergosk. Now the Iraqis themselves are fleeing. Erbil is trying to absorb these terrified men and women who have abandoned their towns and villages, taking with them only what could fit in a bag, carrying their children, trying to find a place to stop and regain a semblance of calm, to breathe and drink some water and try to believe they will find a solution for the days ahead . . . Erbil is expanding, cracking on all sides. And in the street, on the women's faces, what she sees is the grip of fear.

"We cannot stay here, Your Excellency . . . " The sound of airplanes is coming closer. "We have to hurry, Your Excellency . . . " The plane swoops down. Everyone in the tiny cave freezes. The strident sound of engines in a dive. And then gunfire, everywhere above them, shattering the rock, exploding in their ears. It is as if the earth were trembling. Another plane is following, already. Soon they'll be bombing. They have been hiding in this little cave in Aya for two days; they concealed the entrance with a silk curtain and the cave is full of the heavy smell of the incense they have been burning day and night for the dead who fell at Maychew. When the first bomb explodes one hundred meters from the entrance the priests around Haile Selassie begin to pray. "Your Excellency . . . quickly!" So he gets up, surrounded by these men who have been watching over him as attentively as a mother, and they rush out of the cave. Run. Lose your breath. Run before the planes finish their circles in the sky. Feel the stones slipping beneath your feet but keep on running, flat out. Run, because that is what the vanquished do.

Assem went into the archeological museum. The man at the ticket counter repeated insistently that for him the visit would begin in one hour, at the café across the way. He didn't reply. This is the appointment he has been waiting for. He has an hour to kill. So he walks around the tombs in the first room. There is everything in Beirut, antiquity and frenzy, ruins and dollars. He looks at the spouses' majestic sculpted faces on the lid of the tomb, they lie side by side but slightly raised on their elbows; how serenely they plunged into death, leaving the world to its noise. And the bas-reliefs below them are a mêlée of bodies, swords, combat. Greeks against Trojans. It is war: the blows delivered, the severed bodies. He looks at this commotion of death—the cries and moans, and then these spouses looking so calm, while the crowd swarms just beneath them. Will he enjoy such serenity at the moment of his death, like some Roman patrician? He hears the shouting welling up within him. He remembers. The road between Sirte and Misrata, and the dictator was there, a few meters ahead of him. The crowd all around were yelling and stamping their feet, and they did not yet know whether they wanted to escort the man or pull him to pieces. He remembers. Overexcited bodies paying no attention anymore to the blows they deliver. Assem would have to get a bit closer there to see him, Gaddafi, or rather what remained of him, bruised and wild, his face distorted, eyes blackened, his lip split; Gaddafi had lost all resemblance to the arrogant lord Assem had met a few years earlier during the dictator's state visit, where he slept at night in his Bedouin tent in the courtyard at the Élysée Palace, humiliating his host, France. He remembers. How the voices around him saturated the air. He had to act like everyone else, shout and adopt the same abrupt, violent gestures, just to keep his place there, in that first circle of an enraged people. The spouses of the museum in Beirut look so calm. Can they not hear the cries of the crowd, the slurred words Gaddafi is still trying to say, promising them gold if they would let him go in peace? Can they not hear the firing of automatic rifles expressing joy at the capture of the dictator? He thinks again of Leptis Magna, he had wanted to visit the site a few months earlier, back when he was an instructor for the rebels, and there, the firing of heavy weaponry seemed incongruous. They were so small, so insignificant with their struggle to bring about the fall of Tripoli. The Roman columns overlooked the sea like steles of time, and next to their immobility the cracking of weapons could only seem ugly. At the time he had felt, as he feels today, that he belonged to this other era, an era of urgency and war, where action was called for, and he had left the site with the same sadness weighing upon him as now, as he leaves the spouses behind on their catafalque; they watch him walk away and back out into the danger of the Beirut streets, into the heat and noise and the tiny concerns of one life among so many others, while they go on staring at eternity with a smile.

Get away. Run, head down. He is just a rat fleeing from the eyes of the Italian eagle that wants to devour him. He will remember this all his life, these long days spent hiding in the shelter of vegetation or in villages. For a long time he will remember these nights when they had to keep marching, relentlessly, toward Addis Ababa. He ordered his men to make a detour through Lalibela. He was able to go down into the rock-cut church, a jewel of Christendom in Africa, and he prayed. What did he ask God, there, in the shadow of this cross-shaped church dug into the ground? What did the rat ask? Now he knows—and will remember all his life—what it means to be trapped, to be hunted by the victors, and have only a god to talk to, while outside the men are anxiously watching the sky, not daring to interrupt him during his prayers but hoping those prayers will not last too long, because they mustn't linger. There is nowhere he can stay. He is constantly having to strike camp. He advances during the night, while Marshal Badoglio and the Duce sleep in silk sheets, dreaming of supremacy amid odors of mustard gas.

At UNESCO's request, the French Institute in Erbil has arranged a small office for her. It's hot, but she is glad to have a place where she can hold her interviews. Several people are already waiting in the corridor. Word has gotten around that there is a lady who is looking for information about the museum in Mosul. The first visitor is a young man who asks her if she can find a place for him and his family to spend the night. She tries to explain that she cannot help him, that this is not why she is here, that this is the wrong place to ask.

"Just a place for me and my children . . . "

"I'm sorry. I don't deal with that."

"I'm from Mosul."

"When did you leave?"

"A few hours before they got there. I didn't want to leave, but there was no other option."

"Do you know what happened at the museum?"

"They're destroying everything."

"Did you see it?"

"Everything, like I said. Everyone saw it. That is why they came. To kill us. And raze the city."

She can tell she won't learn anything from this man. The more he speaks, the shriller his voice. He is getting agitated. His hands are trembling. She knows there's nothing she can do for him. So she gets up and thanks him for coming, wishes him good luck and lets him go back out into the chaos of a city that is searching, calling out, running this way and that for something to drink and a place to sleep.

"Tell them to repeat that. Tell them there's still time to bomb the train." The radio officer resends the message. General Graziani waits, tensely. He cannot believe Mussolini would refuse. The Negus is there in that fugitive train. They can intercept the train, reduce it to rubble, finish him off. Is he hesitating? The General knows what must be done. This is no time to dilly-dally. If he managed to find Omar Al-Mukhtar in Libya, it's because he knows you cannot dither. Isn't that why the Duce chose him? He hounded the leader of the Libyan uprising until he had him in the palm of his hand. He offered him amnesty in exchange for his surrender, and when Al-Mukhtar refused he ordered to have him hanged. And it didn't bother him one way or the other. As it would not bother him one way or the other to bomb the Negus's train. They are blacks. Finish them off. Does the Duce want to reconquer Ethiopia the way they reconquered Cyrenaica and Tripoli, yes or no? He is getting impatient. Still no answer. The train is getting away from them. With every second that goes by the Negus's chances of survival are increasing. He doesn't like it. This is not the way you win wars. The radio crackles. The soldier listens attentively, then turns to him: "The answer is no, sir. They said to let him escape." In any case it's too late, thinks

Graziani, disgusted. The Negus has gotten away from him. Will he learn, someday, that his life was decided at this very moment? Can he, seated comfortably now in his compartment, imagine that his fate has been decided? He will flee across his country, trying to reach his capital, oblivious of the fact that there were eagles in the sky that circled over him for a moment then decided to leave off their circles and vanish.

The men who were waiting in the corridor have left. Maybe they overheard her say that she could do nothing to help refugees and went to try their luck elsewhere. There is only one old gentleman, with a neatly trimmed white beard, wearing a jacket that is too warm for the temperature in the corridor. But he hasn't removed it, and it doesn't even seem to bother him. There is some dust on his shoulders. "Dust from Mosul . . . " she thinks, and feels moved. The city is so close. He enters her office, timidly. He doesn't look her in the eye. She greets him and asks if he is from Mosul. He nods.

"You know," she says, "that I'm not here to help refugees. I work for the Iraqi museums."

He looks at her with a certain expression in his eyes, as if he were about to own up to a misdeed.

"I live across the street from the museum," he says quietly. "Sometimes the guard gives me the key when he knows he can't be there to open in the morning. It doesn't happen often, but sometimes he gets held up . . . "

"Do you know anything about what they have done?"

"I saw them arrive . . . from my window."

"You were still in Mosul when they arrived?"

"Yes. I left the first night. I was lucky. Now, it's harder. But my son is courageous and the first night he found a way."

"The museum?"

She doesn't dare ask her question. The man looks at her and continues his story.

"They showed up in three four-wheel drives with loud-speakers. They declared that they were taking possession of the city, and that the artwork in the museum was sacrilegious. A few of them went inside. You could hear them making a lot of noise. I think they smashed everything . . . "

"Did you see them take any objects out of the museum?"

"No."

He is still hesitant. Then, his voice almost fearful, he adds, "But I took this." And from his jacket pocket he takes a little package wrapped in cloth and sets it on the table. She looks at it. He lowers his eyes. She opens the package, gingerly. Inside is a pair of earrings from the Sumerian era . . .

"I went in at night. There were still some guards outside but I know a way in from the back, to the meeting room. I didn't go to the main room of the museum, I was too frightened. But along the corridors there were a lot of broken vases. And this . . . So I took it. Not for me. You understand? But I thought it shouldn't stay there . . . "

She thanks him. Tells him how important it is, what he did. She says again that he acted wisely, and praises his courage. He gets up, still a bit awkward, then disappears without a word.

He orders a *café blanc*. He is sitting on the terrace of a little café just opposite the museum. He observes every passerby, every car that goes past. He eavesdrops on the conversation at the next table, between two elderly men, until they get up, say goodbye to the owner, and leave. He tries to make the most of such moments because he knows they are the last calm moments he will know for a long time, but he already feels the tension in his body. In his mind he recites verses by Mahmoud Darwish, to delay the moment when he will once again be a professional, a French intelligence agent who for ten years has been carrying out missions of targeted assassination, here in the Middle East, or in the Sahel. "Will you die in Beirut . . . "

but he doesn't remember the rest. His mind is too distracted by the people in the street. He can feel the tension rising inside him. He ferrets deeper into his memory: "Beirut/The night . . . No night denser than this," and he remembers Mahmoud Darwish, how twice he went to see him, once when the Palestinian poet was in Paris, at the Hôtel Madison, opposite the church of Saint Germain des Prés. He had found him at the bar, alone. It must have been eleven o'clock. He introduced himself, hesitantly: should he make up an identity, say that he was a bookseller or a professor or something? He still remembers: the moment he approached him, the man looking at him, and then he knew he would not lie, and held out his hand and said, "Monsieur Darwish? I work for French intelligence . . . but I would like to know if you would be willing to talk with me about poetry for a few minutes?" And the man did not shudder or even seem surprised. He gestured to the armchair across from him. Assem sat down and they spoke. "If this autumn is the last, let us apologize, for the breaking and backwash of the waves . . . " They talked, and Darwish didn't ask him anything personal. Just as they were about to part, as they were shaking hands, the poet said these words, looking him deep in the eye: "Don't let the world steal the words from you." He pictures him there again, with that face of stone, and this is the first time he has thought about that moment. It was years ago. And he has to confess that he has let the world steal the words from him. There have only ever been acts. Action takes over everything, leaves no room for anything else. Action with its intoxication and intensity, leaving everything else so insipid in comparison. What good were words in that crowd on the road between Sirte and Misrata, while he was gripping his 9mm, ready to shoot if the situation got out of hand, and Gaddafi's face there a few meters away from him, hovering in and out of sight with the swaying of the crowd? What use were words when no one could hear anything but shouting and gunfire and the crowd going wild with joy? No one was in any state to speak or to listen to any words, and Gaddafi looked like a floored boxer, or a battered woman. All you could hear was the crowd yelling as they pushed and shoved, and the Kalashnikovs fired in the air to celebrate the dictator's capture. He feels as if he is about to lose his words again. In a few minutes someone will show up, surely armed, and take him to the place where Job is hiding. Danger is imminent; he must be on his guard. They may decide to kill him now, on this terrace, to send the message to France not to get involved, that they know perfectly well that it is the Americans who have sent him, or simply because Job has gone crazy, and wants to destroy everything around him. Assem must be vigilant, on edge. Words no longer have a place and yet he clings to them, does not want to let them go. He knows that he is more himself when he keeps his words inside him, or that in any case he is closer to the truth of the world. Again he sees Darwish's face, remembers the line, "My homeland, a suitcase," and then suddenly, superimposed upon the poet's face in his memory is the face of the young Kurdish combatant, Shaveen, as she was when he saw her for the first time, outside the entrance to the camp at Kawergosk, where he had gone to get her in the pickup. Shaveen, one of a group he was there to train, and who, when he had asked who she was fighting for, had pointed to the refugees' tents and said, "For them." And he had envied her her strength. Who was he fighting for? The interests of France? Yes. But those interests changed so often . . . Before he found himself on the road to Sirte, among the crowd screaming madly with pleasure at having the tyrant in their hands at last, he had been in charge of protecting Gaddafi . . . But Shaveen did not hesitate. Her face was the face of victory. That is what he told himself: he envied her because even if she did not manage to halt the advance of Islamic State, even if she was killed by enemy fire one day, she could not lose. Something in her would never be soiled, never defeated. She was fighting for the families in the tents who crowd together at night in a fug of human warmth and the smell of charcoal. Whereas he—when could he ever say he had won? He had carried out so many successful missions. Men had been eliminated. But had he won? Words have left him. Every time he has had to immerse himself in the thick of the action, poetry has fallen silent, and Darwish looks at him in the depths of his memory, at the Hôtel Madison; but yet again he has to accept the departure of words, because a car has just pulled up, at speed. Stopping abruptly in front of him. A man jumps out, not even bothering to hide the automatic in his hand. He looks to the left, to the right, opens the back door and motions to Assem to get in.

He resigns himself to leaving Lalibela. They have to keep moving, hide in their own country. The enemy has won. The Italian troops are about to march on Addis Ababa. When will he ever be back here? There are days when he thinks about the possibility of organizing an internal resistance, of fighting every inch of the way. But he knows that Ethiopia needs a political voice, and it is up to him to carry that voice to Europe. So he advances, obstinately, reaches Magdala, then Fiche. There, five cars and five trucks are waiting for him. At last he can sit down and catch his breath. He is a fugitive in his own land. Is he really about to flee? He will be the first king of kings to leave his people behind. When he reaches Addis Ababa he can tell it is no longer even an issue. There is no other option. There is something frenzied about the mood in the capital. His generals tell him: the men are deserting. No one wants to fight anymore. The police authorities tell him that scenes of looting are becoming increasingly common. He mustn't stay here. There is the sound of gunfire in broad daylight. Addis Ababa is panicking, rearing up, going mad. He is no longer in control.

And so he leaves, abandons everything: the palace, the Ethiopian people, his dreams of armed resistance, his valiant subjects; he leaves as a deposed monarch, humiliated by the world that has let him die and never raised a finger, he leaves with his wife for Djibouti, and he stops talking, cannot say a word, he is ashamed, this man, the descendant of the victors of Adwa, he is ashamed and does not speak because now the words have abandoned him.

Sullivan Sicoh stands by the tombstone and gazes at the name etched on it: Jasper Kopp. It's strange to think that this man who saved his life is dead and that they will never meet. He tries to picture Jasper Kopp on his way every morning to Creech Air Force Base, taking his seat in the cockpit with a colleague, shutting himself away like that, for a few hours, from the rest of the world . . . No, not the rest of the world, just the quiet suburb where he lives, the supermarket, the children, and immersing himself in a world of camera images, aerial views, zooms, radio commands. He tries to picture Jasper Kopp staring at the images from the far corners of the earth that reach him after a time lag of only a few seconds, Jasper Kopp flying over Afghanistan every day then going home again at night. He tries to picture Jasper Kopp kissing his children goodnight, gliding over the Taliban mountains, doing his shopping at the supermarket, blowing up vehicles on a straight road or pulverizing the caves where vague shapes have been moving. How much of the schoolyard in Kalafgan did Jasper Kopp see? What were the last images his screen showed him before the explosion? Did he see a child running after a ball? Did he try to go back on the order to fire, or could he only watch with terror as the Hellfire[3] advanced,

---

[3] Air-to-surface missile.

inexorably, to bomb that building and turn him into a mass murderer? Is it possible to say that the two of them were together: he, Sullivan, dragged facedown along the ground by a crowd of angry men, eating dust and kicks, while Jasper Kopp was floating in the sky, his gaze encompassing the houses, then all at once releasing death, launching his missile at the school, which in no time would be nothing but smoke? Were they together? The man lying there beneath that tombstone committed suicide because he fired that day. Kopp was the only one who knew his secret. Can you die by virtue of being too far away from the battlefield? By virtue of killing at the same time you pick out your yogurt? By virtue of triggering explosions with your fingertips while you kiss your children on the brow to wish them a peaceful night's sleep? Can you die from remaining intact, untouched, out of reach of the blows, the cries, the smoke and the rubble? The women screaming in Kalafgan: Sullivan had heard them, whereas Jasper Kopp, that day, heard only the piped music in the supermarket on his way home, and perhaps his wife asking him how his day went. And if she did, what did he reply? Did he say that he saved an American soldier who was about to get lynched? Did he only tell her about that, or did he also tell her that he had wiped a school off the map, and that the mothers of Kalafgan would weep for the rest of their lives because of this cursed day? Sullivan looks at the grave and he knows his secret is there at his feet, beneath the thick moist earth of this American cemetery, and that it will stay there until he, Sullivan Sicoh, decides to reveal it. He will choose the time and the place. And when he does, he knows that Jasper Kopp will at last be able to give a cry of relief from his grave. He will scream the shame that overwhelmed him, pound against his coffin, and that will be good. He will feel the same wrenching grief as the women of Kalafgan, and only then will anyone be able to say that they were truly all together that day, in northern Afghanistan—Sullivan, Jasper Kopp, and the grieving mothers, sharing the same wound, moaning from the same defeat.

He leaves the world he knows. He leaves Africa and keeps his head down, hiding his face to weep in his tiny cabin on-board the *Enterprise*, which sails under the British flag and is taking him to Jerusalem. Haile Selassie has left his country and does not know if he will ever see it again. He has lost the war, but far more than that: he has been humiliated before the community of nations. No one came to help him. He is the first king of kings to leave his country rather than die on the battlefield, and he does not know whether this means that as a sovereign he is braver or more cowardly than his predecessors. His head is spinning. His stomach is in a knot. The coast is receding behind him and with it his authority and his hopes. From now on he will be a deposed king, a king in exile. Italy is celebrating her victory. At this very moment the streets of Addis Ababa are probably being ransacked. He knows there must be chaos, and fear. There will be shooting, and bodies dragged along the ground. Pillaging, killing, settling scores in the cowardice of night. Ethiopia no longer has an emperor. Ethiopia is going mad. And so he too seems to be engulfed by night, the night of exile, and cold, and evenings of despondency where not a single word can bring comfort. The world has suddenly closed all around him, and he is nothing but a little man, anxious to know when it will be given to him to see his country again, and whether that day he will still have the strength to stand on his legs.

She returns to her desk, sits down, and weeps. She thinks about all the artifacts: the ones that will be rescued, the ones that have already been destroyed, the ones that will disappear for years then show up at an auction in London or Singapore.

She thinks again of Paul-Émile Botta, and how he discovered Dur-Sharrukin. Of everything that was unearthed, catalogued, packed in crates. First by Botta himself, then by his successor, Victor Place. Entire shipments removed from oblivion, from the guts of the earth, that were meant to be sent to the galleries at the Louvre. She thinks in particular of the shipment in 1855. Two hundred and thirty-five crates floating down the Tigris on their way to Baghdad. But the convoy was attacked, and the crates sank to the bottom of the river. Only twenty-six were recovered. Two hundred and nine are still there in the gray waters of the Tigris, unearthed from oblivion for a short while, only to return to it almost at once . . . She thinks about all of this. A struggle that seems so pointless, to save works of art while all around her the world is going up in flames, tearing itself apart; her struggle is bound to fail, because all she is trying to do is snatch something from the void that is doomed to return to it. Then her thoughts turn to Assem, and the Bes statue she gave him. Where is he now? Dare she imagine that when he found the statue on leaving Zurich, he carefully took it out and caressed it as if he were caressing the sacred dimension of time? Dare she imagine he has left for Lebanon swearing to himself he'll go back to the statue once he's accomplished his mission? Dare she imagine that he is in a car in Beirut, being driven toward danger? That he might be thinking about her the way she is thinking about him? She looks at the Sumerian earrings, touches them, tries to picture the woman who first wore them, the long dizzying thread that joins her, today, in this city in chaos, to the faraway inhabitant of Dur-Sharrukin, and she knows that these items are looking at them the way Bes, the dwarf god, is now looking at the man she has loved, wherever he might be, and is traveling with him into that danger.

He gets into the car. From the time of his meeting in Zurich with Auguste and Dan Kovac, everything has been leading here: to this moment when he gets into the back of this car, voluntarily placing his life in the hands of these men and women he does not know and who are now looking at him warily. One of them, with Latin American features, searches him, brusquely lifting his shirttail to check he has nothing in his belt. It all happens very quickly. The words have gone. No one speaks. In the front, next to the driver, a young Arab woman sometimes turns around to make sure he is really there. The car pulls away. He is not frightened. He has done this so many times. But he feels as if he is leaving a known world, the world of missions, targeted killings, and secret operations, to immerse himself in another realm. He feels as if he is going deep into a barbarian territory, leaving the torches of the last camp to flicker behind him, while the thick silence of an animal world surrounds him altogether.

V
AL-JNAH STREET

They did not blindfold him. No one is speaking. He looks at them, furtively: the young woman in front of him must be Maria Casales, the Colombian. She has a tattoo on her forearm: a black five-branched cross. The man on his left, the one who searched him, must be Hassan Bahan. He remembers a photograph Dan Kovac showed him in the café in Zurich. He doesn't recognize the others. "Where are we going?" he asks, in Arabic. The driver looks at him through the rearview mirror. A long moment goes by before anyone answers, then finally the driver says, "Job is waiting for you." The car heads south, driving through Chiyah. He knows that the further south they go, the greater the danger for him. The Shi'ite neighborhood of Haret Hreik is not far from here. Is that where they're taking him? The car keeps going, and evening falls over Beirut. He can smell the sweat of the man who is on his right. Their arms are touching. Do they know who he is? Did Job himself figure it out? And if so, did he tell them? They don't seem tense. Suddenly the Colombian woman turns around and says in English with a strong Latino accent: "When he talks . . . You'll see . . . " and her eyes are shining. She says this with a childlike delight, as if she is eager for his sake, envious that he is about to meet Job for the first time. What unites them, these men and women with such different backgrounds? Former members of the FARC, Palestinian militants. Egyptian revolutionaries, Syrians who have fled the regime of Bashar al-Assad. Is it the lure of money? Their own little trafficking? The pleasure of ruling, like this, in a city where their Kalashnikovs serve as both deed of title and passport? The car slows down, leaves the major artery they were on. To the left he can see a billboard. "Welcome to Haret Hreik." Is the fact it is written in English meant to be ironic? What a strange city . . . He is about to plunge into the heart of the Shi'ite neighborhood, "Hezbollah-land" as they call it. How has an American with a little troop of mercenaries from all over the planet managed to gain a foothold in the preserve of Hezbollah?

Kalafgan is far away. This is a new mission. He has reintegrated SEAL Team Six and once again he is Sullivan Sicoh, squeezed into a helicopter as it flies through the night toward danger. Like so often in his life up to now. The wounds have been erased. He is among his own kind, and nothing else matters. There is no fear, in the helicopter. Concentration, yes. Every man in the unit is focused on himself, automatically checking his equipment, tightening the helmet strap one more time or making sure the infrared sight is working, all gestures that allow him to empty his mind, to take some distance from the outside world. They were given one final briefing just before they took off, to be informed of their target. Then they were divided into two helicopters and now they are headed straight for Abbottabad. They are nothing but bodies, the juddering of the aircraft, on their way to Pakistan. Once they reach the scene of the action, they will seize a house whose layout they know by heart. They'll have to be quick. There will be women and children. Bodyguards, and the probability of gunfights. Anything is possible. They have been prepared for every eventuality. And Sullivan Sicoh rehearses these automatic gestures, impatient, like all the men around him, to jump out into the night.

The streets are poorly lit. A tangle of electric wires forms an arbor of black lianas across the main roads. "Have you known him for long?" Assem asks the woman.

"You don't need to have met him often to have known him for a long time," she replies, with a strange smile.

There is admiration in her voice. Does she know that Job is a former member of SEAL Team Six? Does she know that when she belonged to the FARC, if anyone had asked Sullivan Sicoh to plant a bullet in her brain, he would have done it without flinching, because that was his job: to eliminate the enemies of the United States of America? She cannot not know it. What is it that unites them, then, this woman and all the others in the car? He looks at them. These people here are bound to paint a particular portrait of the man he is about to meet. How has Job managed to bring together such a disparate group of people?

They drive through Haret Hreik. More slowly, now. The man on the left, the Palestinian, has taken out a 9mm and is holding it squeezed between his knees. They are not in home territory here. They are tolerated. But they know very well that the neighborhood can close over them, like concrete jaws, depending on political arrangements, alliances, and collapses of alliances.

Hannibal knows—despite the Romans' huge numerical advantage, despite his own soldiers' fatigue—that he is about to live through one of those moments that constitute History. Beneath the helmets and the leather armor they are sweating profusely. The sun pounds down on the colors and seems to cause the trees to tremble. In the distance the sea is motionless. Not a breath of air. The ground itself is hot, and the lizards, probably sensing the unusual drumming of tens of thousands of footsteps, have slipped beneath the rocks and stopped moving. He looks at the enemy lines: the Romans must be at least twice as numerous. Every day they alternate command. Today it is Varro who is holding the standard. That changes nothing. They still fight in the same manner: putting the young recruits in front so they will not be tempted to run away, and the veterans to the rear. Today everything will be different. He knows that if he wants to beat Rome he will have to reverse the normal order of things, the way Alexander did with Darius, at Issus or Gaugamela. He has to be crazy. Otherwise, he will be fighting one battle after the other—some he will win, others he will lose—and in the end, the forces will counterbalance each other. He has to risk more than that. So he orders for the front line to be extended. The Romans must be watching his maneuver. "More," he says. And his own lieutenants begin to worry: if they stretch it too far, the front line could break, and that would lead to defeat. Indeed. It's a risk he has to take. But he orders to stretch it still further. And the line where the Carthaginians are positioned is now much longer than the Romans', but it is also thinner and more fragile. Varro smiles. He must be thinking that Hannibal is trying to make up for the fact he is outnumbered. "The heavy cavalry will charge the center, first," he says. "We have to break up their line." And he never doubts that this is what will happen. He knows the Romans are more numerous. He assumes that it is to offset this disadvantage that Hannibal is stretching his line out as far as he can. He cannot see the genius behind the maneuver because he cannot see the madness. He is lending his own thoughts to Hannibal, the calculations he would have made, had he been in his place. Reason dictates the Carthaginians should not envisage any other plan than to try to confront the enemy and pray they will not be swept away by the cavalry charge. Break through the front. It all boils down to that. And Varro sets his shoulder to the task. He is glad the battle is taking place on a day when he has been entrusted with the supreme command, because this means his name will be on everyone's lips at the Senate.

Hannibal gives his final orders. He is calm. He asks for the name of the river that flows a bit further on: "The Olfanto," he is told. Good. He informs his men that Maharbal will lead the light cavalry, Hasdrubal the heavy cavalry, and that he himself will stay in the center with the Celtic and Spanish foot soldiers. That is where everything will be determined. When the moment comes to give the order to engage, while the Roman consuls Varro and Paullus are smiling because they are eager to get it over with, Hannibal can sense that today is one of those days when the chain of events will be a question of grace. Is it History taking hold of that outcome and writing the world for a few instants, upsetting plans and surprising the living? Or is it luck? The Romans charge. With all their might. They want to avenge the defeats at Ticinus and Trasimene. They want to obliterate the fear which for months has been gnawing away at the city. The Romans charge and Hannibal stays where he is, waiting for the cut and thrust. He has to receive the charge and not break the line. He looks one last time at the four thousand Celtic and Iberian mercenaries with their thick faces, their light eyes, feet firmly planted on the ground, and they watch with fear as the horsemen draw closer. Today they are the ones who will determine History, these men who are not even from Carthage. The impact is terrifying. The horses crash headlong into the wall of defense. There are so many of them . . . Hannibal screams at his troops to withdraw slightly. They have to absorb the shock and let the Romans advance. It all depends on this: make Varro believe that the line is retreating under the shock and is about to break, so that he will advance even further, sending in all his men in the hopes of fracturing the wall at last. The Gauls seem to be holding, they brace themselves against the horses, their shields crack from the force of the galloping horses, they have to hold, and withdraw ever so slightly, in order for the trap to work. And that is what happens. Hannibal feels it coming. This is a smile from the sky. In this oppressive heat that is making the helmets unbearable and causing the men to squint, everything falls into place, as if he himself were showing fate which path to take. The Gauls stand firm, even as they withdraw. The Romans advance, blinded by their strength. They do not see that the defense has not given way. They do not see that they have gone too far in and that now, with one fatal blow, because Hannibal has ordered it, the Carthaginian wings will close around them. This long line, that stretched too far, that only minutes ago seemed to be too fragile, is encircling them. And Hasdrubal's heavy cavalry smashes straight into them, driving holes in their flanks. Varro turns pale. He sees the trap but it is too late. He stammers, wants to react, still cannot believe it, still thinks it's a mere setback, that he'll be able to redress the situation. But the battle is lost. They come to inform him that Paullus is dead. Then he realizes that everything has changed, that this is an eclipse, he has just been swept away and it is not his name that will be spoken all through the Senate tomorrow, but Hannibal's, and with terror.

She asked the director of the Institute if it would be possible to visit the citadel in Erbil. He seemed surprised. And yet he was the one who had suggested it, upon her arrival: "Please don't hesitate . . . Dara knows the site well, and we have a few privileges . . . ", but that had been something of a formality, as if he were already sure she wouldn't have time, and now it is late and the request seems somewhat incongruous to him. He tries suggesting going to the restaurant, rather, but she insists, and her face, while remaining polite, turns impenetrable. So he agrees, makes a few phone calls to summon the man called Dara to the Institute. She waits patiently. She can feel the fatigue taking over. She has spent the day collecting testimonies and they all said the same thing: fear, the deep face of terror with regard to these men whose sudden appearance signifies the eclipse of our world. Everything will be burned. They have come to rule, to seize towns, bodies, minds. She got very little information about the museum, because they spoke mainly about everything else: the parade through the streets of Mosul, the black flags flying, the loudspeakers announcing the new life they would have to lead. Her country is going to pieces: invaded from the north, and ravaged by chaos in the south. She is in a city, Erbil, that does not want to be Iraqi anymore. Iraq will soon be another Yugoslavia: a vanishing country. And she, the woman from Baghdad, will have to find another nationality. Her country is being torn apart like a rag pulled at from all four corners. But did this country ever really exist? The one that was thought up and outlined and drawn by Churchill, Lawrence, and Gertrude Bell? Has it ever been anything but the dream of a country, imposed by authority in a region rife with other tensions, other movements? She is in Mesopotamia. Which did exist. And perhaps that is why she wants so urgently to visit the citadel of Erbil tonight. And when Dara parks his car at the foot of the site and they begin to climb this mound that overlooks the souks, she feels as if she has wrenched herself away from the chaos and tears. She has left behind the traffic, the stories of panic, everything burning around her, and it is doing her good. Evening falls and it is not as hot as during the day. They approach the entrance and Dara begins to talk, probably wanting to act as a guide, thinking that is what is expected of him: to explain, provide a commentary, tell her everything he knows. She looks one last time at the city at their feet—alive, teeming, vibrant with the evening stroll, and then she motions with her hand to Dara, as if to say, "No, thank you," or something like that, and in a hushed voice she says, "I'd like to spend a little time on my own," so that he will understand that she doesn't want anything from him, doesn't expect anything, and she loses herself in the streets of this deserted little town, which is in the process of being restored, like a ghost town. Relieved, she immerses herself in the silence. Once she is in the labyrinth of little streets she can no longer see the city of Erbil or hear a single sound. It is as if suddenly she were elsewhere. The night seems thicker. She walks, and feels a certain weakness progressively taking over her limbs. Something in her calves, her fingertips, her thighs, seems to be giving way. It's not fatigue, it comes from further away. It's her illness, she can tell, taking possession of her, slowly, inexorably. She doesn't want to stop. She continues on her way, through the little streets of this empty town that resembles a dead body, a mud-brick town that seems to be awaiting the return of armies that set out centuries ago. Everything is calm. Is she sinking into death? If so, it is serenely. She thinks again of Darius. Why him? Perhaps because at the entrance to the citadel she left a man who had the same name, a name which, like the objects she tries to save, has come down through the ages. Darius, defeated at Gaugamela, pale before the vigor, genius, and beauty of Alexander, fleeing the battlefield, abandoning his wife and children to come and seek refuge here, in Erbil, before continuing his flight to Samarkand. This ground, here, has known so many vanquished men. Those who watch as their world disappears and then discover to their astonishment that there is nowhere to hide. She thinks of all the excavations that have tried to unearth the past—what for, in the end? Do the living have time to learn about the past? Are they not wholly engrossed in the intense, daily struggle to live? And yet, at the risk of his own life, the old Kurdish man she saw this afternoon rescued a pair of earrings . . . She does not know if she will have the strength to go back. She thinks that she ought to sit down and call out for help, but she doesn't. Her head is spinning. Her ears are buzzing. Her field of vision narrows. She puts one hand on the façade of an empty house and tries to breathe calmly. She knows she must be turning pale. But she stands firm. Doesn't sit down, for fear of not being able to move again. Who will hold this town a few months from now? Kurdistan seems to be sufficiently well-armed to resist the advance of Islamic State, but who could have predicted the fall of Mosul? And who knows whether Erbil might not fall one day, too? Perhaps the men in black will plant their flags on the roof of the very house she is leaning against right now? Empires overlap, prosper and fall. The ones you thought had been built to last forever crumble, and in the space of only a few hours Darius no longer knows where to run. Is she about to die? Her body has gotten away from her, this weakness gives her the impression she no longer has any control over her own muscles: is this a message, that she is about to fall? What has she accomplished, then? All her life she has fought for the sake of things that are centuries old, to rescue them from the void, things that should be passed down from hand to hand like the burning objects every generation preserves. And why shouldn't they have the right to the sand, to the earth, to burial? Is that not the fate that awaits all the women and men who are rushing about at her feet right now in the souks of Erbil, whether they are refugees or not, whether they are Iraqi or Syrian? Is this not what she herself will experience: burial, oblivion? She falters. She still has time to think about the Bes statue that Marwan gave her and which she slipped into Assem's suitcase: she is glad she did. It is like placing one of those objects back into the circle of life. Not in the way she has been doing for the last twenty years: preserving, protecting, studying. No: placing an object back into Chance. Will the Bes statue be destroyed? Will Assem sell it to an antiques dealer? Or lose it during one of his trips? It hardly matters; the Bes statue is once again subject to the whims of fate, like an object floating along a raging river, and that is good. She can hear a voice calling behind her, a voice she does not recognize. "Madame Mariam? Madame

Mariam?" As if the town itself were calling to her. No. It's Dara. She understands. Dara must have seen her falter. Dara is running toward her, and he cries out as she slips in a faint to the ground.

The pilot has just warned them that they are about to arrive in the area. They all take deep breaths. In a few minutes they will be in the heart of the action. In a few minutes they will find out if this house is the right one. Later—but it seems such a long time—the day will break and with it the revelation of their defeat or victory. In a few minutes they will know, and Sullivan Sicoh adjusts his helmet, taking his time, cool-headed, ready to do what he has been learning to do for years: strike, and vanish.

Now the car is heading toward the sea. Assem can hear a plane taking off in the distance. According to his reckoning, the airport is to the left, further south. People are leaving, propelled into the sky at hundreds of miles per hour, and in a few seconds they will see the city retreating below them, growing smaller and prettier, because at this distance those gleaming little lights no longer show you how squalid the neighborhoods are. But he is there, deep in those lifeless streets, abandoned by the world. He is afraid. He can feel the palms of his hands turning damp. The car reaches the coast. Al-Jnah Street. They are near the airport. He knows this fear, knows he must let it settle inside him, because it can be useful. It will give him instinct and vigor. It will make his senses more alert. He has traveled a long way for this moment. The car drives down Al-Jnah Street. All along the side, little concrete houses stare out at the sea, clinging to the land like an anthill. Most of them don't have a proper roof. They have corrugated iron sheets on top, with rubber tires to hold them in place when the wind blows. At some point they will be burned, if the Sunnis from the districts to the north come looking for a fight. And then all at once there is a house that is bigger than all the others. He immediately notices a man on the terrace acting as lookout with an assault rifle slung over his shoulder. This is it. The car pulls over. The passengers get out, except the Palestinian, who stays with Assem. He can hear voices calling in the night. The trunk of the car slams. The little Colombian woman has also taken out a machine gun, and she comes to open the car door, watching the surrounding houses all the while. They motion to him to get out. He inhales the pungent sea air. A deep lungful. He has come such a long way to meet the man waiting in the house, surrounded by this improbable bunch of guerrilleros. He feels calm again. He knows what he has to do. He has rehearsed these moments in his mind so often, trying to antic-ipate every contingency. And now he is eager to meet this Sullivan Sicoh, whom no one refers to like that anymore, Sullivan Sicoh who makes his friends tremble and reigns over Al-Jnah Street in south Beirut like some drug lord or revolu-tionary in his stronghold. He is eager to meet him because he knows his host has also been waiting a long time for him, and he will look him straight in the eye, without a mask. Assem climbs the four steps to the porch without hesitating, without even noticing the men and women who have emerged in the garden or on the balconies like shadows, a veritable army watching over the night as vigilantly as any cat.

The two helicopters hover vertically over the courtyard. They are about to land. The men are ready to spring out the moment they touch ground. Suddenly Sullivan Sicoh's heli-copter is knocked violently off balance. The men are thrown from side to side. They realize something unexpected has hap-pened but they don't have time to be frightened or wonder what has caused the sudden shaking. No time to worry that the helicopter might be damaged and they won't be able to take off again. They have been trained to run to the building that is before them and that is what they do, springing out in little groups, and never mind if the pilot is cursing the fact they nearly crashed, nearly smashed the prop of the other helicopter to bits, never mind, the men are already long gone . . .

One man is standing guard on the terrace. He is older than the others, and has a bushy beard. He motions to Assem to spread his arms and legs. He searches him carefully, then says, "He's expecting you," and opens one of the two shutters on the double glass door, letting him go ahead, as if he, the guard, didn't have the right to go any further and wished he did—avid for the privilege granted to this stranger. Assem goes in. The house is bigger than he imagined. A large central staircase leads upstairs. There is something old-fashioned about the living room. Who used to live here, before Job's men took possession of the premises? There are no side doors indicating any other way than up the staircase. He goes up. Once he reaches the second floor he finds himself in a room where the open windows let in the sea air. At the end of a long enfilade of rooms—all plunged in darkness, all empty, all decorated with old furniture that seems to have been forgotten there for centuries—he sees a light and hears what he thinks is the sound of laughter and a clinking of glasses.

Sullivan Sicoh advances, searching through his infrared glasses for any sign of human presence. He moves quickly. He knows that two comrades are following him like shadows. They are covering him, protecting him. The three of them are united because they can see in the dark, like cats, because they have adjusted their stride and are advancing at the same pace, because this may be the first time they have entered this building, but they already know it well for having painstakingly studied the plans. They are united because each of them has his finger on the trigger, will be ready to fire, without emotion, not even stopping as they make their way. They must advance, reach the spot they have been told, upstairs at the end of the corridor, in the bedroom. They are united by the sound of the gravel in the courtyard crunching beneath their boots, because at the same time they hear shots fired by other members of their unit, they are united because they have no time to wonder what is going on. Sullivan Sicoh keeps moving. This is a manhunt, and he will do everything he must to flush out their prey. The three of them walk close together, up the stairs, down a long corridor to this last door, and behind it they will find the man they have come to kill, the man all of America wants dead. And so without hesitating, not wasting a minute, because his body knows he has to be quick and leave the enemy no time to react, Sullivan Sicoh breaks down the door and enters the room.

"Come . . . come . . . Closer, so I can see what they have sent me."

Assem made his way slowly through all those rooms to reach at last a wide covered terrace overlooking the sea. There are two sofas set at right angles, a table, and an armchair; staring at him with piercing eyes and a smile on his lips is Job, a glass of whiskey in his hand. He speaks with a Southern drawl. Assem steps closer, and now his face is in the light. Before he can even say anything, Job asks, "Was it you who killed him?"

He doesn't answer, caught off guard by the question and the man's good-natured welcome. He tries to see whether there is anyone else there on the terrace, whether Job has a weapon . . . He tries to gauge the height, whether he can jump from the terrace if need be . . . And he can see that Job is examining him, and sees what he is doing. There is what he says, this question in his Southern drawl, there are his open arms, his face in the light with this strange smile—as if none of it were meant for the man there across from him, with his smile almost like a bonze's—but there are also those light, lively eyes that have not missed a thing during his guest's arrival: they are sizing him up. "Was it you who killed him?" Assem hasn't answered, doesn't know what Job is referring to, but Job doesn't leave him the time to speak, he waves his hand, as if to indicate that he can wait. "I'm sure you get asked that all the time, more than anything else . . . I know what that's about. Let's say that's a shared experience for us." And he sits down in the armchair, turning his back to Assem for a moment, almost slowly, as if he wanted to point out that he is not afraid, that he is showing him his back, that nothing in him is attainable. "Whiskey?" He makes the offer but is too far away to serve his guest. And besides, he is staring out to sea, as if under a spell, suddenly very far away from this terrace, from Assem, from the question he just asked or all the ones he will ask. Assem goes over to the little drinks trolley and pours a glass. So that's what he meant. Their shared experience. He's talking about Sirte. The death of Gaddafi. He's talking about it because he, Job, was in on the hunt for bin Laden. And what if he were to ask him the same question? Was he the one who fired? No. He won't ask. What difference does it make? There were several of them who made their way down that corridor in the house in Abbottabad. There were six, or ten, of them in the first helicopter. And ten in the other one. All with infrared sights, all ready to shoot. What difference does it make, basically, whether he was the one who fired? All twenty of them did.

Assem has still not spoken, but he feels as if he has been on this terrace for hours already. He looks at Job. He remembers the photographs he was shown in Zurich, the ones where Job is among his comrades, from the days when he was still Sullivan Sicoh. He looks at him now: he has lost weight, has marked wrinkles on his face, but there is a sort of depth to his eyes that he did not have before, an edginess, a substance. He is bare-chested, wearing a long wooden necklace that could be African, and several rings on his fingers; his hair is messy, uncombed.

"Were you prepared to die that day?" asks Job in a muffled voice, and Assem senses that this question is now a test, and that if he doesn't give an honest answer the interview will be over.

"Yes."

Job pulls a face, savoring the truth, letting it float in the air. Then he adds, "So was I. Naturally. But I could tell it was the last time . . . "

What changed him, during that mission to Abbottabad? Was he more frightened than during the other missions? Was it because of the identity of the man they killed that day? Or because one of the two helicopters had crashed against the wall in the courtyard and he thought he was going to die?

"What makes us follow orders, lieutenant, do you know? You're a lieutenant, right? I served under McRogan, you must know that. I saw Abu Ghraib before anyone else found out about the shit we were up to there. I went on raids in the middle of the night to take out guys we pulled half-naked from their houses, and they died without dignity, shitting themselves, literally. You've done that sort of thing too, I bet. What makes us follow orders, lieutenant? Some people think we get a kick out of doing it. You know we don't. I didn't like McRogan. That is God's truth. But I would have let myself get killed for his sake. I swear. At times like that, if the occasion called for it, I would have stood between the bullet and him . . . Why is that?"

He swallows his drink down in one, then falls silent. So Assem senses he can ask his question, and his voice is soft, almost considerate:

"What are you doing here, Job?" And what he means is, What are you doing here in this city that isn't yours and that will spit you out when it's had enough of you? What are you doing here, in this improbable getup, on this terrace surrounded by revolutionaries who are anything but?

"Ah . . . " says Job, raising his hand, as if at last Assem has asked the right question, and he narrows his eyes mischievously.

Hannibal gazes out at the plain. The sea has not trembled. The heat is gently declining. His head is still full of blows and counterblows, cries, falling bodies, whistling arrows, the pounding of hooves. For three hours men have been killing each other. He gazes out at the tide of bodies around him. All Roman . . . He doesn't know it yet, perhaps he will never know exactly, but forty-five thousand Romans are lying at his feet. Still they moan, sometimes they move, beg to be finished off or cared for, they go on sweating as they bleed. Forty-five thousand dead. His own men's arms are aching from so much bludgeoning. All they had to do was close the circle and slaughter them one by one, all those Romans caught in their net. It took time. And now all that is left at Cannae, on the banks of the Olfanto, is a soft, caressing late-afternoon light, and a tide of bodies. Liters and hectoliters of blood are nourishing the earth. So much blood that the earth cannot drink it all. Forty-five thousand severed, gaping, stinking bodies. A vast slaughterhouse roasting in the sun. Because even if the sun is beginning to set, the air is still hot. It is summer. The stones burn with all the heat stored during the day. Forty-five thousand bodies that will take days and weeks to decompose. There it is, his victory: as ugly as an unspeakable butchery. It is the greatest massacre in History. Never again will any battle be the cause of so much death in so little time. He looks at the men at his feet. They lost only a tenth as many men as the Romans, but they lost the soldiers to whom they owe the victory: the Celts. So he leans down, and from time to time he touches the hand of one of them, stiff with death, because it is from these men that he wants to receive glory. Soon the Senate will hear the news. Soon Carthage will celebrate his audacity. Now and forever he will be the victor of Cannae, the one who turned the order of things upside down. The victory he has been waiting for, for so long, since the day he crossed the Strait of Gibraltar and long before that, even, ever since his father told him how he had taken and held Mount Pellegrino in Sicily, his victory has been there, but he wants to remember that it is the dead who have given it to him. It has always been thus, and woe betide whosoever forgets it. The great battles that people remember: atrocious mass graves with birds circling overhead. Is he proud of this? Of the forty-five thousand Romans lying at his feet? Is it really something to be proud of? He wants to remember the smell of viscera on the summer wind, because if History has a smell, surely this is it.

"Do you like relics, lieutenant?"

Assem doesn't understand. Job's questions baffle him. Even more baffling is the joy with which he asks them. As if he were deeply grateful to be having this nocturnal conversation with him, as if these shared night hours in this house on Al-Jnah Street were an interlude of grace. He must know, however, why Assem is there. He cannot help but know. And in spite of this a burst of real happiness goes through him when he asks his question, as if he were talking to a very old friend. He narrows his eyes and waits for the answer. When he sees that Assem doesn't know what to say, he reaches under his armchair, then brandishes a bone. It's a shinbone. Given its size, it can only be a human bone.

"What turns a bone into a relic?" he asks, his tone serious. "Have you ever wondered? I have. And here's what I think. You need two ingredients: violence, and holiness."

Then he lowers his arm and puts the bone back under the

armchair. From now on Assem knows he has no control over anything anymore, that he will have to let himself be guided by Job, that he is the one who is directing the interview and that he will go on talking until he has maneuvered Assem to exactly where he wants him to be. From now on he knows the night will be open onto the sky, that it will be an infinitely long night, and that he will like this. A strange mixture of decay and power emanates from Job. Gone is the honed body he had in the photographs where he posed among the other members of the commando, but in his voice there is a solid, unshakeable strength. He senses that Job is taking him a long way away from his mission, that at this moment the concerns of the CIA are laughable. He is elsewhere.

"History stinks. Don't you think, lieutenant? You and I both know it, because we still have that smell in our noses, isn't that right?"

Why does he keep referring to Sirte? Because it's obvious he's talking about Sirte. Is he doing this to unsettle him? Or to create some sort of complicity between the two of them, to show Assem he knows where he's been, knows what he's been through? He keeps bringing up that moment. Is it so that the angry crowd will fill his mind and he will again feel the heat and fear of that day? Is it because he has sensed that this is Assem's weak spot, and that what is unfolding here on this terrace is a combat? Or is it because he himself is haunted by similar memories, and he needs an acolyte to be able to confront them?

"You won, didn't you, lieutenant? In Libya, that day. But would you say it: I won? I'm not talking about France, but about you, personally. Did you feel the victory?"

He knows he didn't. There is no need to answer. Assem thinks it over. Has he ever felt the victory? The sense of having fulfilled his mission, yes. During Operation Serval, often. When he gave a fighter jet the precise coordinates of a high value target, heard the aircraft soar through the sky and then, a few seconds later, the explosions in the distance, followed by the radio message, "Target neutralized . . . " But victory? No. As if absorbed by the images he has set loose, Job continues, speaking softly now.

"Have you seen Kyle and Maddox? Those American heroes . . . "

Yes, he has seen Kyle. The sniper, celebrated throughout the country. The man with one hundred and seventeen victims. And Maddox, who managed to make the people hiding Saddam Hussein talk. What is he driving at? That it is unfair for the country to remember only them, and not Sullivan Sicoh as well?

"We chose the shadows, Job. You've known that from the start," says Assem.

Job smiles at his remark.

"No. You don't understand. It's not that I envy them. You know what I see when I look at Maddox? You've seen him, in those powwows of his where he talks about his experiences, with his microphone clipped to his ear? A one-man show. He's like some evangelist. He goes all over the South. Kansas. Louisiana. They're all ready to pay to hear what the genius of interrogation techniques has to say . . . What bullshit. Me, what I see is defeat. His life came to an end the day Saddam Hussein was dragged out of the ground, with his hairy satyr's head and his huge stash of money. And he knew it right away, I'm sure. He was losing his great enemy. All he had left was lectures in multipurpose meeting rooms and auditoriums. Same thing for Kyle. The American sniper. Yeah, really. The real story is not the number of men and women he killed. The real story is the wretched end he came to. Shot by another American, a guy who'd been in Afghanistan and volunteered in Haiti after the earthquake and came back stark raving mad. That's the US in a nutshell . . . in those two men. One madman kills the other one because the country kills its children. And it's always a defeat. And maybe Kyle even felt a sense of relief the moment he died, because at least that way he would die a hero. Maybe that is all Maddox wants. To be shot and spared all the years ahead where he goes on telling the same story, with his microphone and his bad jokes, to audiences who as time goes by will hardly have a clue who Saddam Hussein even was, or what the hell the US was doing in Iraq in the first place . . . "

"Is that how you felt in Abbottabad? Defeated?"

Job doesn't answer right away. He smiles gently into the night—or is it a grimace?—then turns to Assem and says, "What do we have to offer in opposition to all that, lieutenant?"

Assem says nothing. Just then he thinks of Shaveen, the young Kurdish fighter outside the entrance to the camp at Kawergosk, so lovely, holding her rifle with determination, her cartridges slung over her shoulder. There was a light in her face that made him sense she would never know the melancholy of combat. Was it because of her youth? Or because she believed body and soul in the Kurdish cause? Was it because she knew she was everything her enemies despised: a woman with long black braids who would not wear the veil and who fought like a man? She stood for everything they wanted to suppress, and if she ever fell into their hands they would destroy her. So for her, to be alive was a victory. Every hour of the day or night. When she went to the front, when she came back, as long as she was alive, she was victorious, and her very existence was an insult, a slap in their faces. Shaveen's smile filled his mind, but he didn't tell Job about her. That is what he has to offer, to set against the mediocrity of victory, against Maddox and his pathetic sideshows, his same old jokes and flamboyant posturing, but he doesn't want to speak about her, doesn't want to share Shaveen with Job. He suspects that if he did, Job would tarnish his memory of her and that would be unbearable. Or maybe it is because he knows that the man sitting there across from him must also have clung to faces like that, but has ended up feeling that basically they were no better than all the others, that they were nothing but a stronger wall against defeat; he knows that if he talks about Shaveen Job will smile and explain to him why she cannot protect him from anything—and he, Assem, does not want to be deprived of that image. So, in lieu of an answer, he says:

"What have you decided to do, Job? Play your own game? Set yourself free?"

Job looks at him calmly.

"I'm glad they sent you, lieutenant," he says with a smile. "Because you understand. That means we will have good discussions in the future . . . "

Assem wonders if this is his way of indicating that the interview is nearly over. He realizes he hasn't said any of the things he'd prepared, so he starts again, with his mind on his mission:

"We haven't talked about why I'm here."

"But we have . . . Of course we have," says Job, "in fact that is all we have done." Then after a long pause he adds, "Do you really think the CIA cares about my occasional little traffic in antiquities? It's something else. Didn't they tell you? Of course not. They let you come and have a good sniff around and they figured the less you know, the better. That's an insult to you . . . But I'm grateful they chose you. It could have been so much more disappointing."

Suddenly he seems overwhelmed by a deep fatigue. He sighs. His features are drawn. He stands up and for a long time he looks at the sea in the distance. Assem can no longer see his eyes, but he hears his voice:

"We'll meet again, lieutenant. Since they decided, in a way, to entrust me to you . . . "

Just then, as if everything had been orchestrated in

advance, as if, through some sort of telepathy with the night and with his men, Job could control everything, the Egyptian who had brought Assem in now appears on the terrace. He nods to Assem to inform him that the interview is over and he must go with him.

"In three weeks," says Job, "get a room at the Menelik Hotel in Addis Ababa. We'll continue our conversation. If our words have not abandoned us by then . . . "

He says this last in a melancholy tone, as if he had a presentiment of the disasters to come, but almost mischievously as well, as if he could read Assem's inner deliberations. Assem is startled. He heads for the door, waits to see if Job is going to turn around—is stunned to find he hopes he will—and just as he is resigned to leaving the terrace Job's voice rings out one last time, louder now, almost threatening:

"Remember the bone, lieutenant. And ask your superiors what it would take to turn it into a relic. Zeal. And believe me, you can find that everywhere. Just waiting to spread . . . "

Assem goes out. As soon as he reaches the enfilade of rooms the Egyptian walks right behind him, and he can feel the barrel of a revolver in his back. He is surprised by this sudden appearance of menace. It is as if Beirut were resurfacing. He has left Job's terrace and his deep, spellbinding voice, and now he is back on Al-Jnah Street, playing the intelligence game—plots, trafficking—and it all makes him immediately long for the minutes or hours—he hardly knows which—he has just spent up there.

VI
CAPUA

It's so strange to see your enemy. Not the soldiers in the opposite camp, on the battlefield, the ones who tremble just like you do and scream just like you do, praying that they will stab you in the belly and not the other way around, not those men, who are sometimes boys not even fifteen or sixteen years of age, no, it is strange to see the very heart of the enemy. That is what he is can see there before his eyes: the walls of Rome. On the other side of those walls are the temples of Juno and Demeter, the Forum, the Senate, shop stalls, the villas of the patricians, and the squalid brothels of the outlying districts. On the other side is the Empire's money and the orders that come and go, circulating throughout Europe. His own men can hardly believe it. Everything is so close now. He remembers the crossing of the Alps and the fog on Lake Trasimene. He remembers the heat at Cannae and all those hours of forced march. After Cannae, when they went to Capua, the men were able to sleep in beds for the first time in three years. And there too he roused them from their sleep, there too he called them back to war and ordered them to march. Capua has been surrounded by the Romans. For the time being, it is resisting, but before long it will have to open its gates or die of suffocation. He must not lose Capua. It's his only access to the sea. From Capua he will be able to send for reinforcements and alternate his men. From Capua, he can maintain the pressure on his enemy and wear down their nerves. Rome knows this. Everything depends on this. That is why they are besieging the rebel city. The trial of strength is dragging on. To try to break out of the deadlock he is commanding one part of his army and marching on Rome. He knows he does not have the wherewithal to undertake a siege. That has never been his intention. He just wants them to believe he that he does. The Empire's capital must feel threatened. Must believe they are heading for disaster and, therefore, call back their soldiers. Then the vise around Capua will loosen and he'll return to prepare his victory.

How long has he been killing? For how many months has war been wearing this face, a succession of ever bloodier battles? There is nothing else all around him: battlefields and circling birds driven mad by the smell of blood. There are worse things than fatigue and exhaustion. There are worse things than the horror of a hallucinatory nightmare of battle. Than hands still trembling hours after the mêlée, than horses singed by fire, than thousands of dead soldiers in a forest so dense the bullets ricochet as if caught in a lunatic labyrinth: there is the feeling of futility. A battle for no good reason. Today's battle more than all the rest. He cannot share this thought with anyone, but he feels it, and it is destroying him. A slaughter that does not even have the virtue of being decisive. Perhaps, in the end, he does deserve his nickname, "Grant the Butcher." How many men has he sent to their deaths since the war started? How many men have lost their lives because they obeyed the plans he made, because they followed the orders he gave? Tens of thousands. Every day they are dying, and today more than usual. What can he cling to, to keep leading men into battle? To Lincoln? Yes, perhaps. He admires him deeply, the man with the long face. And to the cause: slavery is a crime committed by humankind against humankind. He has said so, over and over. Grant must cling to this: he and his men are the forces of progress. They are the future—the only possible future—of the great country that will be born. But sometimes it seems so little in the light of those rows upon rows of supine bodies, their hair in the mud, skin already turning gray—most of them young men—it is so little . . .

She insisted on stopping off at the museum. It is deserted at this time of day, closed to the public. Which is good. That is how she wanted to see it. The inauguration was held last week. She saw the images on television. She heard the speeches the Iraqi president gave, and the head of UNESCO. What no one said was that now a race has begun. The men in black are destroying everything. Yesterday they flattened Nimrud with bulldozers. Every site they find will suffer the same fate: mallet, angle grinder, or dynamite. Which one will be next? There is talk of the temple at Hatra. They consume antiquity, doom to oblivion sites that witnessed the fall of the Roman Empire, that were there at the birth and death of nations, of civilizations.

Hannibal continues to ride along the walls of Rome, in the hopes that his enemy will panic and call the armies back from Capua in order to defend their capital. Again he asks—he has already asked three times since he got there—whether the scouts have brought any news of enemy troop movements. The answer is no. Rome has seen him, is observing him, is making comments on his presence, but has made no decisions. Will the city lose its composure? Again and again he rides past the walls. He wants to be seen, wants the guards to mention it to their superiors, wants the superiors to call the consuls and the consuls to inform the Senate. Hannibal is there, beneath your windows, prowling past the walls like a cat, relishing the prospect of the pillaging he is about to order, "Hannibal himself has come," "The great final battle is near": that is what he wants to hear, "Recall the armies from the south," "Hannibal is attacking Rome," "We must prepare for the siege," that is what he hopes and again he asks, "Any news from Capua?" and he is told, "Nothing." History is still hesitating and he knows there is nothing for it but to wait and remember that one day, as a child, he promised himself he would make it all the way to Rome, and today he is there, the first invader on the Empire's lands. Yes, let them panic! Let fear confuse their minds. Because he has already accomplished something no one ever had before him.

Tonight in his tent he is weeping uncontrollably, mindful only that no one can see him. Not that he's ashamed, but he knows that tears are a sign of weakness, and he has no right to give his men such a show. A macabre coincidence of warfare has brought them back to the same place: the Wilderness forests. One year ago a battle was fought here, against Lee's soldiers. At the time, the Confederate soldiers defeated Hooker. The dead bodies are still there. And today the torrential rain has reopened the graves, and the men who were fighting could see they were standing on a field of bones. Those who fell, face to the ground, were conjoined with the remains of their erstwhile comrades, who welcomed them with a skeletal smile. He is weeping, his mind still full of the downpour transforming the ground into a muddy field, and the fires spreading from one spot to the next despite the rain, burning the wounded men alive. The Wilderness has devastated them. But when he wipes his face to hide his tears, when he leaves his tent to be among his men, he thinks about Rome. *"Qui vincit non est victor nisi victus fatetur."* He who conquers is not the conqueror unless the conquered admits it. He can tell no one, but as he looks at his men trying to warm themselves around a campfire, hardly speaking, trying to retrieve the sensation of being alive, he understands that defeat is not a question of losses but of movement. You have to keep going. What is at stake is not to win the battle of Wilderness, but to prevent Lee from catching his breath. He is marching on Richmond, the capital of the Confederacy. The Southern general wants to slow down, play for time. He is betting on the elections about to be held in Washington. Without a clear victory, Lincoln will not be reelected and, if he is not, the Confederates will have all the latitude they need to negotiate their insurgency. That is what Lee wants. And that is what they must respond to. All through the camp, inside the tents, there are murmurs that the Union army was defeated today. And why are they saying this? Because there are seventeen thousand bodies lying there in the woods, their faces still lit by the dying embers from the fires? As long as History continues to hesitate he will not be conquered, and for the time being, that is what it is doing. It must be forced. That is why he is ordering his men to get to their feet. Tomorrow the army will set off again and continue southward toward the enemy capital. Tomorrow the army will be on the march and as long as it is on the march there will be no defeat.

She walks through the rooms in silence. Everything is in its place. She counts all the objects once again and recalls that twelve years ago, in 2003, she did the same thing, walking through the rooms first this way then that, but everything was different then: windows smashed, chairs overturned, objects on the floor, display cases emptied. Together with several other people her age who had come to help the director they walked back and forth, discovering the spectacle of the pillaging. She may have been young then, but she still clearly remembers how stunned she was. A great crime had been committed, there before their eyes, a senseless, ugly crime. A crime that went against the enlightenment of civilizations, and together, for hours, they crouched down to pick up the debris, to sweep, to inventory what was missing, but everything was missing . . . More than ten thousand items had been lost. Iraq was a vast playground for dealers of all sorts. They had witnessed the looting and could do nothing. Baghdad was being torn apart. She remembers how angry she was, when the looters had emerged out of nowhere in the blazing city, forcing their way into the museum, helping themselves in broad daylight. She remembers the American soldiers who just stood by and did nothing, didn't budge, watched the organized gangs making off with the riches of her country's heritage. She had gazed on helplessly, like so many others, while the museum was plundered. Like others she had yelled at the American soldiers to get them to do something. The impunity of the looters. That was where her life was born. From that day on, after the dictator had fallen for good, she would devote her life to hunting down the stolen artwork. With Interpol or UNESCO. Whenever an artifact surfaced in the back room of a Swiss antique shop or at the bottom of a GI's duffle bag, they called her. Twelve years. Perhaps that is why today she walks up and down, alone, through the vast rooms of the museum, taking the time to look at everything, in silence.

Grant advances, like a bulldog. He must take no notice of the distraught faces, the pain of the wounded, the doubts. He must take no notice of his own hesitation but remain focused on one thought alone: advance. Whatever the cost, day after day. That is how wars are won. You have to be stubborn. So he insists, forces his men to strike camp every morning despite their fatigue, to march again, fight, die, and keep going . . . History is hesitating, has not yet made its choice. After every battle they have to get back up, regardless of the outcome of the confrontation. Thirty days of fighting without a break, and still History has said nothing. It doesn't pick sides, it can't decide, in spite of the battering he is delivering. Three days after the fighting in the Wilderness forest the two armies face each other yet again at Spotsylvania. The Union forces are twice as numerous, and Grant knows that this is his only trump card, as it has been every time since the beginning of the conflict: flood the battlefield with his troops and to hell with the losses. How else could they survive eighteen hours of fighting at Bloody Angle? Twenty thousand dead in that place alone. The shower of bullets is so heavy, the gunfire so sustained that the soldiers are not so much shot down as cut to pieces by bullets. How can anyone witness this and still be alive? General Ewell collapsed in the middle of the battle. Without a scratch. He had seen too much. He lay on the ground and blocked his ears. He was not afraid of dying—he had accepted the prospect long before—but he couldn't stand the sight of everything around him anymore. It was too much. His mind went. He curled up. Why hasn't he, Grant, ended up like Ewell? What is it about him that *can* bear it? General Ewell will never return from Spotsylvania. The soldiers took him to the rear but he has gone mad and talks to himself. Eighteen hours of fighting and twenty thousand dead. When evening came, Grant tallied the numbers. He can't help it. He wishes he wouldn't do this, he knows it's pointless. He smokes his tenth cigar of the day and does the figures, like a demented man: that makes one thousand one hundred and eleven casualties an hour, so that's eighteen dead per minute, or three dead every ten seconds, times eighteen hours . . . He's the one who has orchestrated all that, and he hasn't gone mad?

In one display window she recognizes a few of the lost artifacts. Six hundred and thirty-eight items that the US Army gave back to Iraq after the looting in 2003. And yet, for two years, these items were nowhere to be found. General Petraeus's services certified that they had sent the crates, and the museum insisted that they had not received anything. She persisted, with the help of Interpol, hounding David Petraeus's offices to get them to send her the proof of shipment. Nothing. The artifacts had vanished. Not a trace. And then finally one fine day in 2010 the crates were found. The boxes containing the artifacts had been stored by mistake in a warehouse full of kitchen equipment. She did not know, that day, whether to cry for joy or weep with rage. Two years lost. Six hundred and thirty-eight priceless artifacts stored among the hot plates and worktables. Now they are here. The Baghdad museum is on its feet again. It is a response to the bulldozer in Nimrud and the angle grinder in Mosul. For twelve years she's been fighting art trafficking, for twelve years she's been trying to stop the hemorrhage of Iraq's archeological heritage. So many artifacts will disappear. The men in black are marching on Hatra. The looting will go on. Then a thought comes to her, and she suddenly wonders whether she is not going mad. It feels as if she is walking back and forth, up and down through the deserted rooms so that the items will look at her. So that they will see that, yes, there are men and women who care about their conservation. Who are keeping watch over them. That the world that removed them from the earth is not only a place of rapaciousness and violence.

After Spotsylvania, they have to keep going. He orders his men to march, and they come upon Lee's army again at Cold Harbor. No one knows yet who has won and who has lost the overland campaign. They have already left forty thousand dead in their wake, but up to now it has served no purpose. And in Cold Harbor he makes a mistake. It won't cost him his life. It won't even cost him the victory. A mistake that changes nothing, or almost nothing regarding the evolution of things, it won't even stop him from continuing to progress, to advance southward and put an end to this long march of thirty days of horror outside the walls of Petersburg. But now he knows what the men are murmuring in their camps in the evening:

"The Butcher." At Cold Harbor, in the space of seven minutes, he sent seven thousand men to their deaths. There are no more limits. He no longer thinks in terms of lives. If he did his tally now he would learn that this amounts to more than sixteen dead per second. It's like sending cattle into machine gun fire. Sixteen dead per second. Every man who falls had a life, with his own history, the village where he was born, parents who are waiting for news; every one of his men was afraid but charged anyway because there was nothing else to be done. Now he knows he must accept the name they have given him, "the Butcher," he accepts it and from now on he will hear it everywhere, murmured in his ear, transforming joy to shame and moments of calm to harassment. He will hear it when Lincoln leans over to congratulate him, "butcher," he will hear it when his wife tries to murmur in his ear that she loves him, "butcher," he will hear the crowd screaming it when he marches by, right up into his old age, "butcher," every second, "butcher" at every light-filled moment when he wants to be glad he's alive, "butcher" because the seven thousand dead at Cold Harbor served no purpose. He accepts the name, "butcher," and he will always remember it, even when he looks at the defeated Lee, and later still, when he is president of the United States, "butcher," yes, he has no right to deny it, he who did not go mad like Ewell. Unless, on the other hand, that's just it, he did go mad, but without realizing it, without falling to the ground: mad, yes, because he has reached such a terrifying point, this place that consumes everything, where only the victory matters and everything can be sacrificed to obtain it.

Who has opened the gates to Capua? How many hours of hesitation and discussion or obedience to what sudden impulse led someone—an official representative of the city or a simple citizen, unable to stand the siege another moment—

to open the gates to the city and allow the odors of the perfume market to escape? There must be a hand gripping the heavy iron bars, a voice shouting to let people know the city is surrendering. There must be a hand turning the key in the lock. Do they realize that they have just caused History to change course? That one empire will fall and another one will triumph? The inhabitants of Capua have allowed themselves to be taken in by the ruse Hannibal was hoping to use on the Romans. He wanted Rome to feel it was under threat, that he was going to concentrate all his forces on the city. The Romans didn't believe it, but Capua did. The city thought Hannibal had abandoned them. They did not understand that the maneuver was merely to loosen the vise that had them in its grip, and that later the Carthaginian leader would come to set them free. Someone's hand has opened the gates. They thought Rome would send negotiators. They thought the Empire would order them to disarm and perhaps even punish them severely with heavy taxes. They spoke about it among themselves and agreed to the idea. They did not think Rome would make them serve as an example. The gates of Capua are open. The long period of hesitation is over, this infinite time during which Hannibal has been going back and forth beneath the ramparts of Rome so that everyone would see him and panic would invade the streets of the Forum. History has chosen, the gates have opened and now Capua is overwhelmed not by negotiation and endless discussions but by anger and punishment. The Romans enter and they ransack everything. So that no city will try to stand up to them ever again. So that no one will boast that they caused Rome to tremble. They enter and they make Capua pay for the nights of insomnia, for their patrician wives' fear. They make them pay for those hours they spent wondering whether they would live or would soon be bodies lying in the cold mud of the battlefield. Capua must bleed, and before long the sweet smells of the Selpasia market will be covered by the heavier, more nauseating smell of warm blood spreading across the ground. When the messenger informs him, Hannibal looks at the walls of Rome one last time. He knows that he will not be able to bring the Empire to its knees at this time. Perhaps he will never see these walls again . . . So he takes his time, then gives orders to withdraw. He says nothing. Everyone around him knows what the fall of Capua means. It is their turn now, to retreat to the south. It is their turn to go through three years of traps and waiting. They will have to dig in, in the hills of Calabria, and live there like mountain boars while they wait for reinforcements. It is their turn to live through a siege. History has chosen. It is their turn to flee with the enemy at their heels, day and night. The victory at Cannae is far behind them. Capua is burning and it is their turn to weep.

VII
GENEVA

ddis Ababa. Why did Job choose that city? This was the first thing Auguste asked him when they sat down on a bench on the promenade de la Treille, underneath the leaning chestnut tree Genevans refer to as a sign of the arrival of spring. "I don't know," answered Assem. Auguste seemed annoyed. They spoke for a bit then went to a little restaurant with a pretty wooden façade on the rue Jean-Calvin for their appointment with Dan Kovac. The American was expecting news, wanted Assem to tell him whether Job was insane or not, whether he represented a threat, was preparing an attack against American interests, or was in league with enemy agencies, or whether his mental state indicated he was in any way a security risk. He wanted Assem to answer all his questions but the first thing the Frenchman said was: "He talked about relics . . . "

Kovac looked annoyed, just as Auguste had.

"What did he say, exactly?"

"That for a bone to become a relic, it requires zeal, and he knows where to find it . . . "

There is that long-ago day when they stormed the house in Abbottabad. In the helicopter on the way back, no one says anything. All the members of the commando team are silent. They know that as long as they are in Pakistani airspace anything can happen. Two aircraft came to help with their exfiltration. They had to leave the crashed helicopter behind, in the courtyard, and they blew it up before they left the site. That all took time, and made noise. Abbottabad has woken up. The Pakistani command is certainly in the process of giving orders and it's anyone's guess whether they won't try to intercept the American helicopters, to indicate their displeasure . . . There is that long-ago day, in the aircraft, when they clench their jaws and count the minutes. And then at last the pilot informs them that they have just flown over the Afghan border, and all at once they go wild with joy. Some remove their helmets, give a shout, hug one another. But Sullivan Sicoh doesn't move, he leaves the exultation to others. The mood in the helicopter is one of victory, there are words of congratulation, relief, and pride, but he doesn't shout, doesn't smile. His mission is not over.

When Assem says "relics," Kovac pinches his lips and frowns. Assem goes on, talking about the place where they met, the personal bodyguard, the way Job looks like he's in charge of a gang of smugglers. He tells Kovac that Job seemed "perceptive" to him. He uses the word and sees that Kovac looks surprised. What more can he say? That he is eager to see him again? That he is afraid of only one thing: that at the end of the meal Kovac will get up and thank them for their help, and inform them that the Americans will take over and deal with the matter themselves from then on? He does not want to be shunted aside. He thinks again of his appointment in Addis Ababa and he wants to be there. "Don't let the world steal your words," said Mahmoud Darwish. Is this what binds him to Job, makes him eager to see him again? Is it because—strangely, with his murky, unsettling behavior—Job has put words back into the world?

"Can you give me more detail?" says Auguste eventually. Before asking his question, he waits for Dan Kovac to come back down from the toilets—looking as if he is about to take the entire little spiral staircase with him along the way.

"If you want us to go on with you, you'll have to tell us a bit more. No one believes these stories about trafficking in stolen artworks. Even Job seems to know why you sent someone."

Assem knows Auguste is going for broke now. If Dan Kovac balks and won't tell them anything, his mission will be over right then and there and he'll never see Job again. The Americans will mount an operation to pick him up in Addis Ababa and he'll be found strangled in a hotel room with all the clues of a sordid petty crime—a prostitute after his money, a sexual game gone awry . . . Unless they take him back to the States. Then he'll begin a lifetime of debriefings, interrogation, incarceration, and always the same questions, repeated a hundred times over, until he goes mad or manages to hang himself. Assem holds his breath. He is aware now how much he wants to see Job again, and this surprises him.

"It's tricky," says Kovac in a hushed voice, and Assem exhales, because if the American is giving them an answer it's because he wants to go on working with them. "You know that after we eliminated bin Laden, there was a problem with the body. The sort of corpse that burns your fingers a little and you don't really know what to do with—"

"What does that have to do with Job?" interrupts Auguste.

On the bridge of the aircraft carrier the wind is blowing, swelling waves that are as calm and powerful as hills rolling one after the other. The weather is fine. Sullivan Sicoh looks out at the horizon. He has just joined McRogan, who is wearing his dress uniform, smoking a cigarette while he waits for the imam to be ready. Sullivan says nothing. Before long the imam appears with four sailors in tow, carrying a wooden crate. They come closer. Flags snap in the wind. There are no birds in the sky, they are too far from land. The imam begins the ceremony. They have asked him to make it as brief as possible. The body has been wrapped in a white cloth. Sullivan has not left it even once since Abottabad. Samples were taken to verify his identity and compare the DNA. He recalls the shouts of celebration at the base in Afghanistan when the results of the tests confirmed it was indeed bin Laden. And then the whole world found out. There was an outpouring of joy all over the country. For ten years an entire nation had been calling for revenge. And now there is nothing left but ocean. When the imam finishes his prayer, Sicoh and one of the sailors seize hold of the wooden plank and lift it above their heads. The body begins to move, sliding along the plank, faster and faster, propelled by its own weight until it seems to leap then fall past the hull of the huge military vessel. For a few seconds it is suspended in space, then they hear the splash of water and nothing more. Sullivan stares out at the vast, shifting ocean, rumbling, rolling. He wonders what the ocean thinks of this body they have just entrusted to it, and how long it will take to dissolve it . . . Then all of a sudden McRogan's voice rouses him from his thoughts, cracking into the damp air:

"Well, gentlemen, let us go get our medals."

Dan Kovac has paused for a moment. He must be wondering what he can say and what he must keep quiet, unless it is all an act, unless it has all been thought up ahead of time and he is hesitating simply to make it seem more natural, to give them the impression they are coming closer to the heart of the matter and that once he has said his piece the French will know everything.

"Sullivan was in charge of protecting the body. He was one of the men on the *USS Carl Vinson* aircraft carrier. They held the ceremony with McRogan and a few authorities and then they tipped the body overboard."

"And?" asks Auguste so that Kovac will get to the heart of the matter.

"For a few months, nothing. And then one fine day Sullivan

disappears. At first it looks like a depression, something like that . . . But then a few months after his disappearance there are rumors of some strange negotiations. This intel crops up, in several places, according to which there's an agent offering relics of the al-Qaeda leader to certain jihadist groups. At first everyone thought it was a joke. It was ridiculous. Until the day a Jordanian agent assured us that he had seen the DNA tests and that the guy in question really did have a piece of bin Laden in his possession."

Assem remembers Job brandishing his human shinbone on the terrace of the house on Al-Jnah Street. He can hear his voice, muffled, veiled, almost coy. Is this really what it is all about? Dealing in body parts? A bone to be put up for auction?

"You've got to be kidding," Auguste broke in. "You can't be serious. Even if he managed to steal a finger, a toe, or who knows what, you don't expect me to believe that that's the reason you've set up this whole operation?"

Very calm, the American looks at Auguste. Then he says: "I can understand why you might see it that way, Auguste. But it just so happens that my superiors are not finding this business the least bit funny, nor is the White House. If little pieces of bin Laden start showing up all over the place, it will be hard to keep a lid on things. And there's something else. If Sullivan really did do this, he's too far gone for us to get him back, and I'll be the first to insist I'm not at all comfortable knowing he's in Beirut or Addis Ababa or who knows where, in the process of reaching out to all the scum on the planet. Al-Shabaab and Al-Qaeda in the Islamic Maghreb and the Al-Nusra Front and Islamic State and Boko Haram: it won't take long for one of them to come to the conclusion that a former American commando who's gone off the rails could be an interesting asset, don't you think?"

Assem has stopped listening. He is mulling over what Dan

Kovac has just said. "He's too far gone . . . " He knows that's it. Job is too far gone to come back. He doesn't want to. He is communicating one last time from the far shore where he's decided to land, and that is what fascinated Assem all through their meeting. Job has left life behind. He has cast off the burdens that other men shoulder and is confronting obscurity. If this story about relics is true, it's no big deal where Job is concerned. All anyone should read into it is Job's way of thumbing his nose, his declaration of war, or rather, his way of bidding farewell to his own side. Because after this—Kovac said as much, and Job knows it—he won't be able to come back. He is burning all his bridges. And with a smile, while he stares hungrily into the dark, because from now on he will have no other option, he can only go forward. He is moving away from the world, away from everything, but he is probably getting closer to something that is more genuine, more intoxicating, and Assem knows that this is why he found Job so fascinating and why he wants to see him again, because he envies him for being able to immerse himself like that, with his bridges burning as he stands between the two shores, alone facing the unknown.

"I, Haile Selassie I, Emperor of Ethiopia, am here today to claim that justice which is due to my people, and the assistance promised to it eight months ago, when fifty nations asserted that aggression had been committed in violation of international treaties . . ."

He has waited a long time to be able to say these words. When he entered the great auditorium of the headquarters of the League of Nations on the shore of Lake Geneva, he thought it would be a solemn moment, and he had prepared for it, but instead he was greeted with whistles and catcalls. Italians, shouting at him that he was a monkey, that Italy could not decently sit in an assembly that admitted countries like that. They were noisy. They laughed, made faces, insulted him. There were four or five of them, in the section reserved for journalists. He clenched his teeth and waited patiently for the police to intervene and evict the fascist activists. But it took a long time. Defeat. Right to the end. And the humiliation that went with it. They would leave him nothing: neither solemnity nor silence. In order to remain impassive he concentrated on memories of his country. Standing there at the rostrum of the League of Nations, before the entire planet, humiliated like some common politician you heckle in a marketplace. He is a deposed king, in exile. Even Switzerland only authorized him to come to Geneva once he had promised he had no intention of remaining on Swiss soil. He will return to Bath as soon as he has delivered his speech. To Fairfield House, a little way outside the town, to that house overlooking the road and which is so damp that the empress has to keep a shawl over her shoulders all day long. And before long autumn will arrive, then winter. He will have to stand fast, far from his country. Will he ever see it again? To stockpile the anger he needs he focuses on his memories of the battle of Maychew. "Pickaninny!" The journalists continue to insult him. The police have arrived to surround and expel them but they are resisting, and the more they sense they are about to be thrown out, the harder and faster come their insults. The emperor remains erect, impassive. To the end of his days he will never abandon his astonishing composure, even amid the turmoil of coups d'état: stay calm and you'll give nothing to the enemy. He looks at the journalists, there must be four or five of them, as ugly as the cowardice of the strongest. Do they even have the slightest idea of what happened at Maychew? Of the courage the Ethiopians showed? Would they have lasted five minutes in that machine gun fire, those swine with their ridiculous gestures, the better to ape him? They spit in his face. Mussolini has sent these troublemakers to strip him even of solemnity. So be it. He will endure. He thinks of the villages the Italian air force massacred with their clouds of gas that no one could do anything to prevent; he thinks of how his fighters panicked when they understood that their courage would be wasted, that the enemy did not even need to show his face and they would die there on that battlefield, without glory, amid the squalor of battles that are lost from the start. He thinks of the corpses swollen like helium balloons, all the gassed, disfigured faces. He thinks of all this and is filled with rage. Calmer and calmer. Colder and colder, but he could break the rostrum in two. All the delegates watching him there today, fifty countries are there, some of them laughing because of the scene the Italian journalists are making, others who think it's an outrage—they all represent countries that allowed Ethiopia to perish. They sold their souls to purchase peace. And they don't want to hear what he has come here to tell them, because they know it will be a reproach. It was only a month ago that he fought at Maychew. One month ago, holding a machine gun amid an indescribable chaos of flames, gas, and bursts of gunfire, and here he is today, waiting motionlessly for the four swine to leave at last and for silence to return, and only then, looking them right in the face, those fifty countries who are not his friends, who will applaud out of politeness but will let him go back to the damp city of Bath without lifting a finger, only then will he speak and say these words he has been waiting to say for so long: "I, Haile Selassie I, emperor of Ethiopia, am here today to claim that justice which is due my people . . . "

Assem walks along the right bank of the lake. The May sunshine is glittering on the water. He sees one luxury hotel after another. He leaves the center of town behind him. He wants to walk out to the former headquarters of the League of Nations, which he has never seen. When he reaches it at last, he is surprised by how small it is. Facing the lake, a garden terrace makes the building look like a grand manor house. He tries to imagine Haile Selassie arriving on the day he made his famous speech. The League of Nations never got over it. The Negus buried them. Or rather the League buried themselves, because they were cowardly, because not one of the member countries was ready to fight for a small state. Is it so different today? He remembers the days of waiting when France was pressuring the US to intervene in Syria. He walks farther on his stroll along the lake.

"Have you won, lieutenant?" He hears Job's questions, that nasal voice with its veiled threat, its feverishness. Has he won? For ten years he has been coming and going all over the globe. One mission after another. But as part of what? A war? When he walks through the streets of Paris he doesn't feel as if he is at war. Whose soldier is he, then? In this era when France is neither at war nor at peace, where the threat is diffuse and ongoing, what sort of victory can there be? The vengeance of the state, yes, that he understands. He worked on the assassination of Mullah Hazrat, checking the precise coordinates of his whereabouts. And when the fighter jets bombed the house, he thought about the ten French soldiers who had been killed in the ambush at Uzbin four years earlier, and he felt good—not victorious, but bolstered by the sensation that only fulfilled revenge can bring. But where is the victory when everything just goes on as before? Has he ever known victory in an entire lifetime of operations? A victory that would truly put an end to a state of war, and lay the foundations for peace? What is he doing, then, if it is all just an endless succession of missions? For years he had a deep, sincere conviction he was serving his country. That was how he saw it. Can he actually say with certainty today that he has never taken part in what were dubious police operations? Job's question keeps going around in his mind: "Have you won, lieutenant?" In that crowd on the road to Sirte he never felt the victory. The dictator was five yards away, in a stupor of pain, his face bloodied; Assem felt no compassion for him, but he was not overjoyed, either. And yet the people had been set free. In the end, that is the only thing that is just, the only cause worth taking up arms for: to set a people free. Has he ever worked for such a cause? He walks along the river and imagines the Negus addressing the entire world, gathered there in that building, speaking about his country that had just been invaded, and superimposed upon that image is the one of Shaveen smiling on the road to Kawergosk, in the pickup taking them north to the Sinjar mountains. Why does he think of her so often? Perhaps because she had victory in her eyes. What words can he, Assem, use to describe what he is doing at the moment?

Now they listen to him in silence, probably hoping his speech will not last too long, because they're in a hurry to get back to their hotel, to walk along the lake and forget, as quickly as possible, this unpleasant moment when a little man not five feet tall, the deposed emperor of a faraway kingdom, told them what they were. They listen to him in silence and the Italian journalists' obscene shouts are forgotten. It is his words that reign over the assembly. He talks about the mustard gas that was sprayed onto the Ethiopian troops, and even outside the combat zone—on cattle, villages. Total war to terrorize an entire country. "These fearful tactics succeeded. Men and animals succumbed. The deadly rain that fell from the aircraft made all those whom it touched fly shrieking with pain." He tells them everything, and it takes time. But he will spare them nothing. It is not pity he asks for but they have not yet grasped this. " . . . All those who drank the poisoned water or ate the infected food also succumbed in dreadful suffering . . . " He can see them, those suffering bodies, before his eyes. He knows he might have been one of them. The silence in the assembly grows heavier. Something is vibrating in the air that has nothing to do with the compassion one might feel for the vanquished. And the little man, in his impeccable uniform, speaking perfect English, stands so straight you would think no one had told him that his army has been defeated and his country invaded. " . . . That is why I decided to come myself to bear witness against the crime perpetrated against my people and give Europe a warning of the doom that awaits it, if it should bow before the accomplished fact . . . " The delegations look up with surprise at the little man. A warning? Did they hear him right? His voice is firm. Then they realize that this is no defeated king who is speaking, standing there before them to beg for alms. Is History hesitating again? He continues his speech, feeling stronger and stronger. Nothing can shake him now. He belongs to the lineage of King Solomon. What can Badoglio and Graziani do against him? He belongs to the lineage of the Queen of Sheba and it is not a petition he has brought here today. The delegates begin to sense this and they listen more attentively. The emperor standing before them is a gravedigger—not of Ethiopia's grave, but of the League where they are sitting. That is what he is saying. " . . . I assert that the problem submitted to the Assembly today is a much wider one. It is not merely a question of the settlement of Italian aggression . . . It is collective security: it is the very existence of the League of Nations . . . " And on he goes, responding blow by blow to past silence, to the desertions and false promises, to the blockade that was never lifted, to the multiple little instances of backstairs cowardice. " . . . It is the confidence that each State is to place in international treaties. It is the value of promises made to small States that their integrity and their independence shall be respected and ensured . . . " Now everyone is listening. The man standing there before them is no longer weeping over his country, he has just signed their death certificate, and he is the one who looks strong, much stronger than any of the representatives here. Yes, he has lost everything, he will go back to Bath tomorrow and Switzerland will be relieved to see he has not tried to stay on the shores of the lake, because they would not have known what to do with such a burdensome guest. For three more years he will be cold and the empress will have had enough of constantly catching cold and will move to Jerusalem, leaving him alone to count the days and follow nervously the upheavals of war, hoping that England will grant him the possibility to go back to his people. He will be cold, he will wait night after night, but right now he is standing before them and telling them that they died there with him on the battlefield at Maychew, even thought they'd been congratulating themselves on not taking part in the battle: " . . . it is international morality that is at stake," and when he says this, everyone understands, he says that it no longer exists, that back there everything died. To finish his speech he asks those present what they are prepared to do for Ethiopia, but he knows that the answer will be "Nothing," he knows that the people listening to him have just dissolved into their own hesitations and that is what he came to tell them, that they have lost, without even realizing it, that the League of Nations no longer exists, because henceforth no one will believe in it, and when he leaves the room amid applause, for the first time since the night he fled Addis Ababa he will feel something resembling victory, as if that long hymn of defeat he just uttered had swept away the insults and told of invisible joy yet to come.

He will go to Addis Ababa and see Job again. The Americans will be there behind him. He will be the bait. Those are the words he must use to qualify his mission. He has to put Job to sleep while the others decide what to do with him. Does that have anything to do with patriotism? Isn't this simply making him a dubious sort of cop? Private militia, negotiators, former agents gone over to private security companies: countries at war are full of them. Is that how he is going to end up, too? In some oil-producing country where he'll sell his know-how to major French groups who have been dazzled by his feats of arms? Of course that didn't make him what he is. That is not what he likes. He wanted to be *in* History—not that it should acknowledge him (that's not his ambition), but to feel it, to be in those places on the planet where it is seeking to leave its mark, thrashing about, hesitating, taking terrifying, excessive forms. To feel its breath, to see how it shapes countries, distorts lives, creates singular spaces. That is what he has always wanted. And he has often felt that breath of History. During Operation Serval, or when he was an instructor in Kurdistan, even in Sirte, when it was History shaping Gaddafi's swollen mask. He felt it in Afghanistan. Sometimes it was frustrating, sometimes it was terrifying, but he was there, at the pulsing heart of events. And the headiness of witnessing how a simple decision at a precise spot can change everything: that too he has felt. He knows that Sullivan Sicoh has also known that feeling, and loved it. That is what they have in common. And that is why he made the appointment with him in Addis Ababa. Because basically they are brothers. And never mind if he knows—cannot help but know—that when they meet, there will be a trap. Job invited him to that second meeting to tell him how alike they are. He too has known those moments when time stretches out, when seconds grow longer and History hesitates. He too has pressed the trigger on his gun, three bullets, a dull thud, a body falling, the body he scarcely had time to see, it went quickly, it always goes quickly, it happens with tension, without emotion, but there is neither fear nor joy, because there's not enough time, three shots and the entire world will know a story has come to an end, ten years of hunting the terrorist who defied the United States of America, and it will be said of them that they were heroes, but they know that everything could have changed the moment the helicopter landed in the courtyard of the house in Abbottabad, with that sudden loss of balance, the rotors breaking, they would have found the bodies of dead American soldiers, Pakistan would have demanded an explanation, Al-Qaeda would have rejoiced, they know that everything always hinges on tiny little things, the pilot's reflexes, the muscles in one's wrist, bringing the copter down in spite of everything, and the gesture that saves them leads them straight to the three shots because the moment the helicopter lands History makes its choice and all that's left is to follow the path it has laid before them. Basically that is what he loves. The moments when History hesitates. What has it decided in Job's case? Does any of this have the slightest importance? No, probably not. Because Job is only fighting for himself. He would like to know what History has chosen for Shaveen. That matters, yes . . . Maybe, deep down, it all disgusts him? It's as if they were forcing him to look at who he is, at what he thought he would never become. Maybe this is the sign of defeat: this feeling of awkwardness with regard to oneself? He will have to ask Job if he really did steal a bone from bin Laden's body, and if so, where he is hiding it. He will have to talk and act as if it were important, although to him it is not. He never wakes up wondering under which dune in which part of the Libyan desert Gaddafi's body is buried. Alexander the Great's, yes. Hannibal's, too. Because they had a vision, because those are the bodies of men who saw History abandon them, when they could have reigned over it, because they were men who brought down worlds and gave words to new worlds. Job knows this. And in all likelihood if he really does have in his possession a shinbone, a finger, or a rib from the Saudi terrorist, it must immerse him in an even greater melancholy, because he is wrong and he knows it. It doesn't take only zeal to make a relic. The remains must have belonged to a man who caused other men to tremble, first with surprise, then impatience.

VIII
PARIS

S itting on the exam table, she buttons up her blouse. The doctor has examined her breasts. His hands were cold. She was startled. Then she concentrated, as if she wanted to see what his hands were feeling, to search with him for the enemy, encircle him in her curves, make him feel her desire to live, to resist. "You have to think about yourself a bit more . . ." said Dr. Hallouche, looking at her through his glasses with a kindly smile. Now he is looking at her records. "You are going to need all your strength for this fight. Do you have support, from friends and family?" She doesn't immediately answer. Support? Yes, she does. From all the men she has loved. Those whose names she remembers, Marwan, Assem, and those whose names she never knew. Yes, she has support. The statues she's handled. Assyrian jewels. The great colossuses of Khorsabad, which are there inside her, because this is her life. And Botta is there, too, Mariette Pasha, Hormuzd Rassam, is that something she can tell him? Is that what he is asking?

Night is falling on Addis Ababa. Mount Entoto is slowly disappearing. There is not a breath of air. Assem returns to the Hotel Mekonnen on foot. The humidity is everywhere—on the bodies of the women in the market, on the facades of buildings, in the unceasing commotion in the street; there is humidity in the gazes of passersby and the fatigue of children. He feels sad and is in no hurry as he walks because he does not want to get there too early. He does not want to lie down in that empty, soulless little room, with the ceiling fan his only clock. He does not want to wake up tomorrow morning in a sweat—humid . . . humid . . . enough to make your body melt—and go to his appointment with Job. It's going to be ugly. The Americans will be in position. He has just come from a meeting with them at the embassy. The tone has changed. They are not asking him to evaluate Sullivan Sicoh anymore. They are not asking him to have an opinion. He is the bait and that's all. They spent twenty minutes explaining what would happen: they will leave him the time to say hello and have a little chat, but before much time goes by he'll have to find a way to get outside. At which point he will confirm that Job is indeed there, then all he'll have to do is vanish and they'll take care of the rest.

She was silent for so long after Dr. Hallouche's question that he understood. He doesn't ask again. With his sensual Lebanese features, his broad hands—when he was palpating her she had not noticed they were so big—he is now telling her about the protocol and what it implies, what they are going to do to her body. He is speaking softly, as if she were a child, and when he has finished he smiles and says, "Do you have any questions?" Yes, she does. Am I going to die? Does she have the right to ask that question, the only one that she is, literally, dying to ask? Is she going to die? Yes, of course she is going to die. That is not how she should frame it. Soon? Is she going to die soon? But she says nothing, she restrains herself and quietly says "no." So he picks up his appointment book and says, "When can you come back? We should start as quickly as possible." And it is as if he were answering the question she didn't dare ask. So she opens her diary, gets a bit muddled, and suddenly Cavafy's lines come back to her: "Body, remember, not only how much you have been loved . . . ", and in addition to those lines it is Assem's voice that fills her, the precise texture of his voice, the rhythm of his phrasing: "Body, remember . . . " and it fills her with strength, it is as if he had just embraced her and whispered into her ear, for her alone to hear, something that is right, not comforting, not cheerful, but true. So she raises her chin and Dr. Hallouche sees a determination in her that surprises him, and in a firm voice she says, "Next week, whenever you like."

When he reaches Haile Selassie Street, a car pulls up to him. The driver leans out the lowered window and says, "Taxi?" He waves him away and the car slowly moves on. He keeps walking. His thoughts return to Sullivan Sicoh. He remembers when Job talked about Chris Kyle and Eric Maddox, the heroes of the nation who had come home, back to civilian life, their bellies bloated with beer, their evenings spent at the bar telling the story of the attack near Fallujah for the umpteenth time, their eyelids drooping, their voices ever furrier. Job's voice had been filled with disgust. Maddox and his lectures, his microphone clipped to his ears, his shirtsleeves rolled up to his elbows, pacing back and forth onstage as if he were doing stand-up and punctuating his stories with well-worn little jokes. He had talked about all that and in his voice there was terror. Was his decision to go back and forth between Beirut and Addis so he could get away from that civilian life? To prolong the danger so he would never return to life as it used to be? Because he could tell that peace would finish him off, even more surely than a night in a helicopter in the Afghan sky? Assem understands. He remembers his last trip to Iraqi Kurdistan. When he went to train young Shaveen's group. On the way back he had a stopover in Vienna. He remembers the hours he spent in the terminal . . . He had just left Erbil and the Kurdish training camps. He had just left Shaveen's upright gaze, Shaveen who was fighting because her sister had been kidnapped by Islamic State during the capture of Mount Sinjar. He had just left the refugee camps, all those mothers with exhausted faces looking at their children playing in the mud, cursing their inability to offer them anything better. He had left all that behind, and scarcely two hours later, all of a sudden as he disembarked, his jacket still redolent of Kurdistan, there were the duty-free shops as far as the eye could see, and Viennese waltzes for background music in every corridor. It was December, so of course there were toys on display everywhere, and fake Santa Clauses too . . . He'd been paralyzed, he didn't know what to do, couldn't speak or eat a thing. This was the same world. Barely a two hour flight away. The same world: there was a saleswoman with her hair in braids and a ridiculous Tyrolean dress showing off her cleavage, so that businessmen would stop and buy a box of chocolates or a sausage wrapped in cellophane, and that saleswoman lives in the same world as Shaveen with her automatic weapon slung over her shoulder, or the barefoot children in the camp at Kawergosk, who haven't realized yet, because they're still too little, how their mother is fading away with every day that goes by, and soon she won't have any smiles left. This is the same world, an ugly world for having such differences, side by side. And the blond-braided saleswoman imperceptibly tapping her foot to the rhythm of the supermarket waltz has no clue that Shaveen exists, just as the *Peshmerga* have no time to think about the fact that somewhere there might be a place with piles of watches in plastic boxes, and sausages sold to the swirl of waltzes. To move from one world to the other is the hardest thing. And perhaps that is what finished Job off . . . After the night in Abbottabad, after the aircraft carrier and the ceremony where the remains were thrown to the sea, they were asking him to go home, to his Michigan backwater, so he could shake his neighbors' hands, drive his pickup to the nearest breakwater, and fill up his fridge with yogurts?

How can anyone do that and not be torn from some small part of oneself with each passage from one world to the next?

Hannibal doesn't say a word. He hasn't spoken to anyone in two days. The swell is causing the ship to pitch. As far as the eye can see there is nothing but gray sky melting into the metallic color of the sea. He is leaving the Roman coast to return to Carthage, abandoning his victories and his legend. The Romans are no longer trembling. At what point did fear change sides? Was it when Scipio managed to capture Cartagena, taking with him an enormous booty of gold and equipment? Everything had always depended on what would happen there, on the Iberian peninsula. It is the key to this total war that has spread from Gibraltar to Greece. For a while he and his brothers had thought they would be able to unite the two Punic armies, his own and Hasdrubal's. He was meant to come down off the hills of Calabria to head back north, and Hasdrubal would land his ships north of Rome and march south. But Hasdrubal lost at the Metaurus. And he is there, now, at his brother's feet, on the deck of this salt-sprayed ship, in that stinking sack. He is there, returning to his native land, defeated. Neither he nor Mago will see Carthage again. Hannibal had his brothers' support in battle but now he is taking them back to their mother, in pieces. One day his men brought him a wicker basket sent by the Romans themselves, and that day tore his soul open. In the basket was Hasdrubal's head, unrecognizable, his face swollen, his mouth dry, his hair soiled with mud. They sent him his brother's head to unnerve him, to make him go wild with rage, to drive him mad. He has had the battle of the Metaurus explained to him dozens of times. He was told that when Hasdrubal knew he was losing, he charged straight at the enemy. He didn't want to survive his defeat. He knew only too well that if the battle of the Metaurus was lost the two armies would never be united, and that if they could not do that, it would be impossible to conquer Rome. So he charged straight at the enemy lines, to die in battle. Mago too perished. He fell from his horse, his thigh pierced through. His men managed to get him away from the battle and onto one of the ships anchored off Genoa, but he died onboard, carried off by a fever in an unbearable stench of pus and incense. Hannibal thinks about his brothers, and about this war that has devoured those he loved most, and he remains silent, for only silence can shroud so many dead.

Assem walks through the streets of Addis Ababa; often, as soon as he is out of earshot, a child turns around and tugs at his mother's dress and says, in a conspiratorial tone, "Mama, did you see, the white man . . . ?" He goes on walking and thinks to himself that he is not sure he'll be able to survive the revolution the day Auguste tells him he's done a good job, and that he doesn't have any other missions for him just now, he can go home and get some rest. He would like to talk about this with Job. Tomorrow. In the neighborhood of the Lion of Judah, on the fourth floor of the building where he's expected, but he knows they won't be able to have that kind of talk. They won't be given the time. And the farther he walks, the more he begins to suspect that he is betraying Sullivan Sicoh. And he hopes that Sicoh, with his hallucinatory insight, will have thought of everything. He hopes that Job is using him, using them, using everyone, and will know how to escape.

A military victory. That is what they need. Petersburg must fall. Or Atlanta. One of the two Confederate cities they have been besieging for months. They must fall, otherwise Lincoln will not be reelected. That is what Jefferson Davis and Robert E. Lee are banking on. They are playing for time. If they can fend off a siege until the fall, the Union will vote for the Democrats and a peace treaty will be signed. Only a military victory can save the Union, because everything is getting bogged down, nothing is working. Grant smokes one cigar after the other, he can no longer sleep. To his wife, who writes him letters full of tenderness and concern, he would like to reply that between them lies a pool of blood. He sometimes thinks that the best thing would be to leave her. What kind of life is possible after all this? How can he forget the smell of gunpowder, the sight of dead bodies? He has been at war for too long. Young men have died following his orders. And yet Julia goes on talking to him about Lincoln, exhorting him to cling to the president's words. She must be able to sense that he is losing his way. In all her letters she repeats that History will vindicate them, that the abolition of slavery is considerable progress, but he no longer hears her, does not even reread her letters in an effort to let her words touch him. Everything seems too remote. Only Sherman's letters bring him some calm. Because they speak the same language. In the latest one his friend informs him of the death of young McPherson, a brilliant officer, thirty-three years old, slain on horseback outside Atlanta because he refused to surrender. Sherman wept when they brought him the body. How many more young men like this one will he have to bury? The nation's finest. How many such men might have lived and gone on to lead the country? McPherson had exceptional talents. "He will eclipse Grant and me," Sherman liked to say, to anyone who'd listen, and now McPherson is nothing but a dead body, and you go and pay your last respects, but never again will he serve any purpose. Such a waste. Entire months of waste. He does not want to hear talk of just causes, of fighting for freedom. He cannot take it anymore. He just wants Sherman to conquer Atlanta. Only that will stop the bloodletting. Atlanta must fall, or Petersburg. But for now, nothing has changed.

He crosses the Mediterranean, returns to Carthage, and he knows that an era of politics, with alliances and betrayals, is about to begin. For the first time in thirteen years the initiative to fight is no longer his. It is Rome that is onstage now, Rome that provokes him by sending him his brother's head, the way he had provoked them by burning the land in Tuscany. He has known ordeals and suffering before now, he has known horror, the fear of the battlefield, guts spilling to the ground and men moaning their last, but in the end there was always victory, every time. And that was enough. Never have any of his men wanted to revolt, never have there been any plots or uprisings or insurrection. Not the slightest grunt of disobedience. Even Alexander the Great was abandoned by his men on the banks of the Hyphasis. Hannibal, no. They obeyed him. But henceforth they will begin to fear. Henceforth defeat will be there in camp in the evening, wearing them down every day a bit more. He must lead his army in spite of everything, keep his composure, stand firm. The Carthaginian camp is going to break up. And if he wants to come out on top, he will have to win the other war, the one not waged on the battlefield: he must silence Hanno, and prevent Masinissa from transferring his allegiance. He gazes out to sea with the bag containing his brother's head always at his feet, and he hopes that if he must lose, he too will be fortunate enough not to survive the defeat.

Most of the men go screaming to the front because they cannot do otherwise, they are too afraid. Not Sherman. The heat is stifling. Drops of sweat trickle down his scalp beneath his hat, but he sits ramrod straight on his horse. The men are looking at him to give themselves strength, he knows this. Just as he knows that in these moments of brutal combat, he enjoys the privilege of staying calm. Where this gift came from, he has no idea, but that is the way it has always been. He is mad. He has never hidden it. Everyone says as much: Sherman is demented. Some sort of unhealthy melancholy is eating away at him. He has mood swings and is prone to what his men call "eccentricities"—but not here, never. Under fire, that all goes away. He sees things clearly. And instead of paralyzing him, the danger surrounding him enhances his powers of concentration. He knows this is a gift, to remain calm in battle. Grant is the same. As are all the great warriors of History, those who are capable of seizing an opportunity amid the fray, of finding a breach, reversing the course of events. He is calm. He can see which way the battle will go: everything depends on the railroad line south of Atlanta. So he orders the charge there, because that is where everything can give way.

Assem walks down Haile Selassie Street as night is falling. He is haunted by his uncle's voice. It enervates, exhausts him. It is the last thing he wanted to remember today, but it seems his mind has decided to make him even more distraught. His uncle Damien, professor of international policy at Sciences Po, lover of poetry, who gave him volumes of poems by Pasolini, Darwish, and Césaire, to acquaint him with the rebellious voice of the world. He hears him now, in the dimly lit streets of Addis Ababa, he hears his uncle saying: "A free man, for Christ's sake! That is what your father would have liked." He doesn't want to remember this because it makes him too sad, but he has to, the memory won't leave him alone. He had just informed his uncle that he was leaving for the military academy at Saint-Cyr. He said it with joy, and his uncle, across from him, kept his solemn face and summoned his father's memory: "A free man . . . That is what your father wanted for his son!" And it is like a slap in the face. He does not want to fall out with this man he loves, this man who has raised him since he was ten years old, when he lost both parents to an automobile accident, he does not want to shout, because his uncle has done everything for him and will go on to help him even more, introducing him one day, when he comes back from Saint-Cyr, to a former director of the external intelligence agency; but also, and above all, introducing him to the poetry of Éluard and Neruda. He does not want to shout, nor does he, he simply goes away. They will never speak about it again. His uncle will never reproach him, he will even support him when he can, but that phrase still lingers: "A free man . . . " He has never forgotten. Did he betray his father's spirit by enlisting in the army? Has he, Assem, been free these twenty years, from one mission to the next? And isn't that what Sullivan Sicoh wants: to be free of the army, of following orders, to be free of himself, of everything, and live according to his own lights, in the darkness?

When he anchors off the Punic coast he senses the men's fear at once. The Roman fleet is a few days ahead of him. It is huge, and he's been told it has anchored a bit further to the west, near the Strait of Gibraltar. Carthage has locked its gates. He can see the fear in people's eyes, in the way they greet him. Everyone is thinking the same thing: the wind has turned, and if they did not make Rome yield it is Rome, now, that will devour them. There is talk of an immense armada. Four hundred cargo ships carrying men, horses, food, and arms, escorted by forty warships. No one has ever seen such a thing. Rome has raised her head and is coming to strike. He says nothing, clenches his jaw. Those who believe that everything is preordained are wrong. He must get home as quickly as possible to prevent Hanno from spreading doubt, and convince the men that nothing has been lost. For thirteen years they have been waging a war of empire. Did Carthage really think they could go to war without suffering? Or subjecting only their soldiers to suffering? Now it is their turn to feel the sting of attack on their territory. And why shouldn't they? Their villages will burn the way the villages in Tuscany burned. Civilians will tremble, hoping never to be in the path of the armies. War will be everywhere. But he knows how to wage it. They have suffered so much already, enduring ordeals that no one could have imagined—forced marches, nights spent shivering, the Alps and the dark massifs of Calabria, they have been through so much, but there is one thing he is not accustomed to: seeing fear in the faces around him. Every time someone comes up to him, greets him, that is what he sees— not the fear that goes before a battle, not the fear of pain or death, no, but a darker fear: the fear that all these months and years of battle will end in defeat.

Sherman catches his breath at last. The Confederates have finally yielded. They have retreated and are entrenched in Atlanta. What begins now is something else. To make a city fall is an ugly matter. It is like strangling someone with your bare hands. It takes time but there is no more uncertainty, because however much the victim thrashes and flails, he can no longer save himself. You see the mouth of your enemy open and gasping for air. You see his eyes grow wider, you feel life, muscular and nervous, struggling, trying to get away, to escape the pressure. He knows how to do this. And so he is choking Atlanta, bombarding buildings and streets, cutting off supply routes until the city falls. At last. A great calm pulses through him. Is there still room for joy? Does Grant in his tent outside Petersburg shout with relief when he gets the telegram bearing the news? Only silence is possible, a great silence of exhaustion. Sherman walks among his men, curtly congratulating the artillerymen, and he makes ready to enter the ruined city. In a few days he will receive a letter from Grant, who is perhaps the only one who knows how much he has willingly given of himself to this war: "Dear General Sherman, Your victory is the most important any general has been able to obtain throughout this war. History will acknowledge that your campaign was led with incomparable—if not to say, unequalled—talent and skill," and he will think these are strange words to describe strangulation. But he does not need to read this letter to know that with the fall of Atlanta Lincoln has just been reelected. He does not need to know that Grant has ordered a salute of one hundred rifle shots to be fired from the walls of Petersburg in his honor to hear the joy of his camp and the first signs of victory. He says nothing, but that is because he knows it's not over yet, even that, strangely, the worst is yet to come. He will have to hound the enemy, harass them. Something is under way now and they are closer to victory, but—he knows this and he is sure that Grant knows it too—it will be ugly, even uglier than anything they have accomplished thus far.

On leaving Dr. Hallouche's building she obeys an urge to stop in a café to catch her breath and relax. She sits at a table and orders an espresso. She doesn't think about anything, tries simply to empty her mind, pays no attention to the passersby. Then suddenly her gaze is caught by the TV screen at the back of the room. Images from her country. She cannot hear the sound but she recognizes the place. Hatra. So it is still going on. The museum in Mosul was not enough for them. They are advancing, and wherever they go, they smash statues and dynamite ruins. She never thought she would live to see something like this. They are advancing and obliterating the sites one by one. Nimrud. Hatra. With mallets and bulldozers they are pounding ancient walls, toppling stones that had resisted, all this time. And when there are still temples or palaces standing, they mine them with dynamite and it all goes up in smoke. She looks at the images on television. It is all getting mixed up. The eras, the shouting, too. The shadows of Nimrud's Assyrian princesses wandering through the dust, holding their heads like wailing women at a wake. The archeologists of the past beat their breasts and heap insults on the barbarians. She can see them—Hormuzd Rassam, Max Mallowan, all those who spent days digging in this dry earth. They are torn apart by the force of the blasts. The dust settles and what remains is a catastrophe. The statues' faces are disfigured, columns lie on the ground. Not archeological sites anymore, but vacant lots. The earth has submerged the vestiges. And suddenly she remembers that little artifact from the Pergamon Museum in Berlin, covered in cuneiform writing. Her stupefaction on seeing it for the first time, as a young woman. The label on the display window gave a rough translation of the ancient inscription: "If you should find this object, put it back into the earth, put it back and go on your way, it is not made for the light but for the kingdom of eternity." It had stunned her. That object, which begged the living not to take it, was now on display in a museum showcase. Was this her profession? To steal items from the void? To go against the will of those who had conceived them? The temple at Hatra: would it not have been better to have left it under the earth? Like the tombs of Philip of Macedon or the Valley of the Kings? We break and enter into the world of the dead, we seize artifacts and offer them up to the carnage of the living—shovels, bulldozers, dynamite . . . It's unbearable, she doesn't know what to do anymore. The tears come. And rage. The thought occurs to her that the next site will be Palmyra and it makes her sick, so she tries to calm down, thinks again of Dr. Hallouche's question: "Do you have support?" Less and less. That is what she should have answered. Less and less if they burn Hatra and Nimrud. Less and less if they take these antiquities from her, this legacy that until now had no fear of time.

He has waited so long for this moment. Three long years of cold, damp English weather, and walking through cloud and fog, and he's thought of nothing else. At last he is on his way home and for the first time since he fled he will be walking upon the African continent. And yet he is overcome by melancholy: it is not the uncertainty of the struggle that lies ahead, it is not the fear that he might fail to retake Addis Ababa, it is the question that has been haunting him: has he ever been anything other than the plaything of nations? From the window of the hotel where he registered as Mr. Strong he looks down at the Alexandria street below him, teeming with vibrant urgency, and he feels sad. He is on his way home, but it is thanks to the war. The European nations, which had scorned him, have suddenly changed their minds. France and Britain are at war with Germany and Italy, and all of a sudden certain experts have come up with the idea that an exiled king might prove useful, if he can incite his country to rise up . . . He knows that is exactly what is being said in the halls of embassies and consulates. That's the way it has always been. When has he ever been the master of his fate, or his country's? His defeat against Italy was decided when Britain and France refused to lift the blockade. Everything since then has been predetermined and his warriors' courage could change nothing. Now he is making the most of the vagaries of the great war engulfing Europe. Has he ever decided anything? Before long he will reach Khartoum and try to go as soon as possible to Ethiopia, so that people will know the emperor has returned. Every day he is getting closer, but now he has France and Britain to accompany him. Colonel Monnier has gone on ahead, but Wingate is traveling with him like a chaperone. How could he fail to see that he decides nothing? He will regain his country and his throne if the Allies win the war against Germany; therefore, essentially, his fate has always been tied to this: the goodwill of Europe, and the interplay of nations. Ever since he gave his speech in Geneva he has felt nothing but hatred for these diplomatic contortions. He will not say as much; he will remain impassive and behave in a friendly manner toward Wingate, but when he looks down at the Alexandria street below him he knows that his alibi is not appropriate. He should have been called Mr. Weak, because that is what he is: weak, and dependent on Great Britain for his hopes that he might, someday, return to his homeland in triumph.

She has always loved Paris. She remembers afternoons in Alexandria when she would walk naked across the sun-washed room where they had just made love, and she would ask Marwan, ingenuously, "When do we buy a little apartment in Paris?" And they would laugh like two young lovers at the thought of seeing themselves strolling with their arms around each other on the Pont des Arts or down the narrow streets of the fifth arrondissement. Marwan with his slow pace, and she clinging to his arm as if to let herself be carried by her giant, who would often stop and turn around when a Parisian woman walked by, and she would have to scold him with a tap on the hand for showing such a lusty appetite, reminding him that he was married, and that would make them laugh . . . Yes, they had often thought about it. This was before that day when Marwan came and didn't stay, when he looked like a punished child and spoke in a dull voice. He was sick. She had found out later, through colleagues. So that was it, then? Simply this: with the approach of suffering and death he was going back to his wife? Was that it? All the rest was swept away. All the rest had been nothing but entertainment? Would she not be allowed to share in his suffering in some way? By supporting him? And what about her, now, who can she turn to? And is this why she is thinking about him just now? Because if she could, if he is still alive, would she want to go to him? She walks down the avenue d'Iéna, enjoying the beauty of the facades lit by that gray light that turns Paris into a palace of zinc. She is determined to make the city her home. She will work out a schedule with the British Museum. She has just passed the Musée Guimet on her left. She hesitates for a moment, thinks about going in, just to see the Gandhara statues again, in the big room on the ground floor, the astonishing beauty of the buddha with the moustache, his chest covered with necklaces, but then she decides against it, she wants to be in Paris, in the street, without the statue, without history, just in the present moment as she strolls, letting Dr. Hallouche's face fade away, along with his words, "protocol," "fight," "chemotherapy" . . . She wants other words, words that will bring comfort. And then all of a sudden she thinks about last night, and the man who came up to her in the bar at the Hôtel Pullman. It was eleven o'clock. She'd gone down for that reason, because she couldn't stay in her room. She felt like shouting, or running away. She got dressed, put on makeup, wondered if a man would come up to her, and she was both disgusted by what she was doing and eager to do it, a man, any man, just so she wouldn't be alone with her demons, as they say, but there are no demons, just crushing solitude. The man came. She didn't have to wait for long. They began talking. The kind of things you say at times like this, things that are nothing but a rather hasty prelude, because you are embarrassed by the imminent encounter of your bodies, and among the questions that weren't really questions she had said, "What do you do in life?" and there, instead of giving any old answer, he could have said what he liked—passed himself off as an architect or a doctor, it hardly mattered—he went pale and said, "I'm a failure." And she knew at once that from then on it would be awkward and difficult. She knew there would be no night in bed, no pleasure, but it was too late: the man was talking, explaining how he had failed at everything, in every domain, I've been cheating on my wife and she found out, I have a shit job, and on he went, nothing could stop him, a complete outpouring of self, and she had to get out of there, she couldn't take it anymore, she left him sobbing on his barstool with yet another glass of whisky that would eventually put him to sleep, only then would he stop talking. Now she remembers the man and the violent disgust she felt toward him, to the point where she had to get up and leave, without even letting him finish what he was saying . . . She was afraid she might be like him. Losing, failing at everything she does. Her love life, all things considered, has left her on her own; her profession has her running after artifacts that the world simply submerges. Is that what it means, to fail at everything? She fled because it felt like someone was holding up a mirror, that she was the one sitting on that leather barstool, muttering to herself as if she were talking to her whisky glass, her back rounded to hide from the gaze of the world, but that wasn't it, she was mistaken. She is walking, crossing the Seine on the Pont de l'Alma. The light on the water sparkles as if reflecting the rooftops. Paris is there before her, light and silvery, and she knows she has not experienced failure the way that man has. Things have not played out like that. Success or failure: that's not the point. She has succeeded in what she set out to do, where she has applied herself. She has immersed herself in life, passionately, she has struggled and fought . . . Where is the failure? What she does know is defeat, but that is something else. Back there in Dr. Hallouche's office: that was defeat. The feeling that something has arisen before you and it will submerge you and you cannot get away from it. To be confronted with the chaos in the streets of Erbil, that is defeat. And the destruction in Hatra and Nimrud, too. Life is damaging her, destroying what she has built, toppling everything that seemed solid, defeat, yes, when Marwan left her, going back to his wife like a lame dog going back to his kennel, but this isn't failure, and she takes a deep breath because she knows that what she is going through, this physical fatigue, this feeling of being depleted, this loss of the plenitude one can only feel when one is twenty years old, this tiny, imperceptible fractioning of the self that inhibits passion, makes it impossible to feel, makes you less graceful, less euphoric, and without even realizing it now you seem more fearful, more fragile: this is the deep arc of life and not some personal weakness. This defeat is not the result of any wrong choice or error or cowardice, she could let the man in the bar go on saying "I'm a failure, I'm a failure," she has lived and has not failed at anything. But then one day there is the moment of capitulation, and leading up to this, progressively, is the tipping into loss, that second period of life when strength is diminished, where sudden bursts of enthusiasm and astonishment and surprise grow rarer, nothing more, an entrance into a period of defeat that is nevertheless part of all the rest, and which she is going to try and experience wholly, without failing there either, she will try to remain herself, Mariam, right to the end. And while she is walking along the Esplanade des Invalides, she smiles and recites to herself, always the same: "Body, remember . . . ," these words that do her good because they connect her to that man, Assem, whom she loves, a man she may be on the verge of loving more than all the others, because as the months go by his image is expanding inside her, and even if they only met that once during her stay in Zurich, even if they never meet again, he is the one, she knows, who gave her the words she was looking for.

IX
ADDIS ABABA

He decides to cross the avenue. Addis Ababa is a bee-hive of activity. He walks between two cars, their shock absorbers so worn down that the bumpers practically touch the ground; he immerses himself for a moment in the chaos of traffic, then comes out on the other side of the sluggish flow of vehicles. The Americans are in position. He has spotted them. Two outside the building. A third one a bit further along. There must be a few up on the roofs. There is surely a car somewhere, ready to intervene. They are there, the trap is set, and the statue of the lion of Judah looks down on the endless stream of cars and the conspiracies of man with equal indifference.

Addis Ababa is jubilant. He enters his city with Wingate by his side. Behind them march the triumphant men of the Gideon Force: Ethiopians, Sudanese, Kenyans, all mingled together, all in rags, but the crowd can't see that, all destitute, but the crowd cheers them wildly. This war that surrounds them, this war that is causing the world to tremble: the Second World War is offering them victory. The Italians have withdrawn and once again Addis Ababa has its king of kings. They marched from the little village of Um Idla to Mount Belaya where the Gideon Force has its headquarters. They marched and their ranks swelled with each village they passed through, rousing the countryside. They marched to restore the dignity that the League of Nations had stolen from Ethiopia, and today the throngs in the streets are cheering for their Negus, home again at last.

The gloom in the building is restful. Two young boys are sitting on the stairs, avidly exchanging notes or photographs. Scarcely looking up, they let him go by. He goes up the stairs. It is not as hot in here. The men from the commando will follow him before long, that much is certain. They will tell the two boys to go and play somewhere else—which they will do, scrambling to pick up their meager treasure. He knows all this. He has experienced similar moments so many times, in other cities. The car will park opposite the building, engine running, door open. The only thing he doesn't know is whether it will be to take Job away, or to erase all trace of the men who have killed him.

The crowd cheers as he goes by. The city is jubilant. Haile Selassie is back in Addis Ababa, and when he left a few years ago it was being ransacked, Addis Ababa that lived through the occupation and tried to fight back, as on that day when nine grenades were thrown at Graziani, nine grenades that should have killed him nine times over, but it is difficult to kill men who live by blood, and fate is oddly considerate sometimes. Graziani got to his feet, and Addis Ababa, which had been holding its breath, had to bow its head again. Today the city is singing, exulting in the passage of its emperor, with Wingate by his side—and he wonders what a victory is, when no battle has been won. It is thanks to the British that he has come back. He did not put the enemy's armies to flight. Addis Ababa is cheering him but he can still hear the Italian journalists' insults in Geneva: "Pickaninny!" The country may be celebrating the victory, but he feels as if some part of the defeat at Maychew was never effaced, nor will it ever be. Perhaps it was only by blood that he might have truly avenged the affront?

Perhaps he will only truly smile the day Mussolini is hung by his feet on Piazzale Loreto in Milan, like a pig about to be slaughtered? He marches through the streets of Addis Ababa. The crowd screams with joy as he goes by. Now he will reign, he will recover his prerogatives, his court, his people, his power. He will no longer be a fugitive hiding in caves or an exile in the rain of Bath, he will live in grandeur and enjoy the respect of his subjects, and so he is trying to savor this city that is his once again, the warmth surrounding him and that he has missed so much. People everywhere are chanting his name, but he can feel no victory inside, or nothing in any case that is equal to the defeat he suffered, nothing to erase the humiliation at the League of Nations or the endless waiting in Bath, as if defeat always weighed more than victory, as if in the final analysis there could be nothing left in the hearts of men but defeat.

It will take a defeat or a victory. That's the way it is. Hannibal knows this. So many men have died, and they demand to know in which camp History will place them, victors or vanquished. He is about to fight a battle here on these lands he left when he was still a child. An entire lifetime has gone by since the day he took command of the Punic army and crossed the Pyrenees. Years of war and blood, years of thinking, coming up with plans, imagining new tactics. And now he is back at the point of departure: the African coast of the Mediterranean. It is here that the war will come to an end. Everything is in place. Alliances have been forged or broken. Rome has always known how to create discord. Syphax found out about the secret accord between Rome and Masinissa. He flew into a rage and changed sides. For a long time the Roman empire had been allied with the king of the Masaesyli who reigned over western Numidia, but for Scipio this was not enough. He plotted in the shadows to turn Masinissa, the king of the Massylii, and never mind if the two of them were mortal enemies, never mind if, in all likelihood, he had to promise to each of them the other man's kingdom, never mind, even, if Syphax ended up fighting on the same side as Carthage, outraged at the fact that Scipio brought about a rapprochement with his enemy. Everything is in place and History is clamoring for its battle. Peace proposals were presented, and turned down. The time for negotiations was extended as long as possible. Hannibal met with Scipio: the two men spoke in a tent that snapped in the wind. Two hours of talk that led nowhere. Rome does not want to negotiate. And deep down Hannibal thinks that's as it should be. He would be ashamed to sign a mediocre peace agreement. He thinks again of his brother, beheaded, and of all the dead of all the past campaigns, and he knows they would have jeered at him in his nights of insomnia. Did he go through all that simply to sign a worthless treaty inside a Roman tent? It may yet happen . . . But not before he has had a chance to fight. And so he sets out his plans with a view to battle. He will position eighty elephants in the front line. And it could be that the Romans will turn pale at the sight of the mastodons. It will remind them of the forty elephants he had when crossing the Alps, how they poured onto the plain of Ticinus. Behind the elephants he will put the Gaulish mercenaries. They are capable of anything. They proved as much at Cannae. Nothing can make them retreat. Then will come the Carthaginians. He has been thinking about it for days already. And he knows that Scipio is doing the same on his side. He saw it in his gaze when they greeted each other. They spoke, and acted as if they were conversing, but each of them was already thinking about tomorrow's battle.

In a faraway hotel room in the past, Sullivan Sicoh watches as the girl gets up. She walks around the bed and goes into the bathroom, offering her buttocks and the light skin of her back to his gaze. How old is she? Twenty? He watches as she disappears, with her long blond hair. Silence fills the room. He lies there for a moment then slowly opens the drawer of the night table with one hand and takes out the bible. A faint smile passes over his lips. He leafs through the pages at random. Suddenly he freezes. There, before his eyes, he has just found the name that was waiting for him. He knows it will be his. It is so obvious. He mutters the words he has just read. He wants to hear them echo in the air of the little room that still smells of fixed-price love: "Death rather than my life." He smiles again but his expression has changed, as if those lines had been written for him, and then he says out loud: "Job." He pauses for a while, seems to be thinking, then gets up, takes his wallet, and goes over to the door to the bathroom. The girl inside is having a wash. It takes her a moment to hear his voice. When eventually she turns off the water, he explains that he will slide the money under the door, she mustn't open it. She asks him if everything is all right, she sounds worried. She is probably not used to clients paying extra. He doesn't answer and he slides the first twenty dollar bill, as he continues to explain: he wants her to stay there, in the bathroom, and call out to him, that's all, call out several times. She asks him to repeat what he has said, she's not sure she has really understood. He slides two more bills under the door and says again, call him by his name, that's all, nothing else, but do it for a long time . . . Then he lies back down, folding his arms beneath his neck, in the bed that still smells of the effort of their bodies. Then the girl's voice rings out and he closes his eyes to fill himself with it: "Sullivan . . . ? Sulli . . . ?"

Assem pauses on the third floor, catches his breath, tries to make the most of the ambient calm one last time. He takes the little piece of paper from his pocket and reads again: "Last door end of the corridor to the left." He walks ahead, down the corridor. The sounds from the street have faded. When he passes by one of the first doors, he thinks he can hear the sound of a television, or a radio. He goes on, until he is outside the door at the end. He knocks, and waits. Nothing.

Again she says, "Sulli . . . ?" changing her tone, her voice more fearful, shrill.

Assem listens out, knocks again. Still nothing. So he puts his hand on the door handle and the door opens slightly. He can hear the street sounds again, traffic. He goes through the door and sees a vast room overlooking the avenue he took to come here. One of the two big windows is open. There is no one. He walks into the room. Not a single piece of furniture, either. He goes further in, to see the other rooms. Everything is the same. An empty apartment. There is just an old wall-to-wall carpet on the floor, and this open window—a sign, at least, that someone came here not long ago. He breathes calmly, allows himself to be overcome by the silence of the place.

"Sulli . . . ?" On she goes, conscientiously doing what she has been paid to do, calling again and again, changing her tone even when she must be in the process of getting dressed. "Sulli . . . ?" This is what he wanted to hear, in this soulless room to which he will never return: his absence. "Sulli . . . ?" He hears the void he will leave when he has left his life.

The apartment is empty. Assem goes over everything he will not have to do: the false dialogue with Job, the moment he should have used the pretext of making a phone call or smoking a cigarette out on the balcony in order to alert the men waiting downstairs. All of that has just been scrubbed. Job is not here; perhaps he never even came to Addis Ababa. He is

thumbing his nose at them. At him. At the men from the intelligence services who are trailing him. He will continue along
his path of folly, and Assem is glad that it has turned out this
way. And so he smiles, wipes his hand across his face to remove
the sweat, leans out the open window, and gazes at the lion of
Judah across the way, reigning with the immobility of a
pharaoh over a nation of automobiles. He makes a sign with
his hand for the men to come, and they come. He can already
hear them climbing the steps four at a time, still believing there
is a mission, when in fact there is nothing more than an empty
apartment.

"Sulli . . . ?" There is nothing left of Sullivan Sicoh, nothing
but the name still uttered by the girl out of nowhere who will
soon fall silent, the name echoing once, twice more, then nothing. And he knows in that instant that everything has truly
been erased, that he has managed to escape from who he was.

He leaves. No one is waiting for him anymore, and the
Americans won't need his feedback for their meeting this
evening at the embassy. When he steps back out into the street,
the heat outside seems to grab him by the cheeks. The air is so
thick that it is almost hard to swallow. He heads toward his
hotel when suddenly, behind his back, a voice calls to him:
"Sir . . . Hey, sir . . . " Initially he pays no attention. "Sir . . . "
Eventually he turns around: it is a handicapped man in a
wheelchair that must be a hundred years old, with rusted arm-
rests and creaking wheels. The man's feet are atrophied, thin
and twisted like a sickly wood. "Sir!" He is about to turn back
and walk away, to leave the crippled man to follow him a few
more steps then give up, but something in the man's eyes stops
him. Something like complicity, an initiated look. He walks up
to him, takes out a banknote and hands it to him. The crowd
pays no attention, sees no more in the scene than a white man

giving money to a beggar. The man gives a broad smile. He doesn't say thank you. He stares him right in the eye and says, in English, "Tripoli. Hotel Radisson. June 27 at nine P.M." And he adds, as a sort of strange signature, these words that he even finds hard to say: "So lamely and unfashionable/That dogs bark at me as I halt by them . . . Why I . . . Have no delight to pass away the time/Unless to see my shadow in the sun," then he smiles at his truncated quotation, because he managed to say it in spite of everything. He senses that Assem has just understood, and that he will be entitled to claim the money he was promised for this errand. Time stands still. Assem can no longer hear the street around him. He is rooted to the spot, gripped by the words. Job is there between them, invisible, speaking through the mouth of the crippled man. Job is there, playing with Richard III and an Ethiopian paralytic, mocking the men from the US intelligence services. He recognizes his voice, even if it is coming from the lips of the disabled man, who does not know in whose name he is speaking, who probably never even met Sullivan Sicoh in his entire life, has done this simply for the cash they've promised him, but Assem knows these words come from Job and that the appointment is genuine. They will meet again. He will be able to ask him the questions that have been haunting him since their last meeting: What have we achieved? What are we obeying? He smiles, and suddenly feels good, in this stifling city amid this chaotic traffic. He will go to Tripoli. Did Job deliberately set this meeting in Libya? Does he want to test him, see if he has the nerve to go back there? Not because the country is at war, but because of the memories of an angry crowd and a dictator with a swollen face. It's no mere coincidence. Is he taking him to Libya so that he, Assem, will be in a place where he is fragile? Perhaps he wants to see him naked, out of this world, confronted with the memory of his limits, the way he was out of this world in the helicopter taking him back from Abbottabad

with his comrades screaming for joy as they looked at bin
Laden's body there at their feet, in that moment when he felt
the irreconcilable split from the other men, perhaps that is
what he wants . . . Wants him to agree to meet him in the place
where something snapped inside him. Only then will they
speak. And perhaps only then will Assem understand what it is
that gives Job that fascinating gaze that is both feverish and
cheerful, as if he thought the blazing world was ever so amus-
ing, because he had penetrated its secrets.

X
ZAMA

They will do to Palmyra what they did to Nimrud. The troop movements have confirmed that Islamic State is continuing to advance toward the oasis of Tadmur and the ancient city. She has to fight, do whatever she can. All morning she has been trying to reach Khaled al-Asaad on the telephone but with no luck. She is going around in circles in her office, fuming about the elderly gentleman, eighty-three years of age, who cannot be reached. She met him during a course in Syria. "Monsieur Palmyre," everyone called him. She remembers his handsome, noble face, with his white hair and his big glasses that made him look like an Egyptian writer. She remembers his speeches, at the end of the dinner, which he sometimes delivered in Aramaic, to everyone's amazement. He likes to do this. Not to impress the young students, but to allow the sounds of the old, old language to resonate one more time. That is his way of giving voice to the antiquity in humankind. Again she tries to phone him. Someone eventually answers. A young voice says hello. She introduces herself, says she is calling from UNESCO in Paris. She is speaking to his son, Walid. He explains that his father is at the site. That he will tell his father to call her as soon as he gets back. She takes the opportunity to ask about the situation. Walid is tense. His answers are brief. "We're very worried. My father is working very hard, to take every precaution." She voices a few encouraging words, thanks him, and hangs up. Men are working, hurrying about, thinking about how to protect the ruins while the country is burning. There is a world that is straining in its efforts to preserve Palmyra for future generations, and in its midst, men are fighting. And the venerable Khaled is still striding through the site he knows like the back of his hand, speaking Aramaic to the old stones.

Zama will be the name of his victory, or of his defeat. It is time to find out. He gives the order to attack, and the eighty elephants charge, goaded by their drivers. They are headed straight for Scipio's trap, but Hannibal doesn't see it. For the time being he is doing his utmost to make sure his orders are properly transmitted. The collision between the two armies is brutal, like two bears towering over each other. The Romans want to erase the defeats at Cannae and Trasimene. Scipio is fighting to avenge his father and all the consuls before him who lived through the debacle. As for Hannibal, he is on his own territory and he knows that if he loses now even the trees will bleed. The thud and clamor of combat rises from the plain. All of Carthage holds its breath. At a five-hour march from Zama, the entire city is waiting to hear whether it will be plundered or will eclipse the Roman empire. Hannibal does not see that the elephants are penetrating into the lines. Or perhaps he sees it and is glad? He doesn't see that they are penetrating too easily. The Roman velites withdraw, allow the mastodons to advance. Scipio smiles. Everything is going just as he hoped. By reenacting the battle of Cannae he will defeat Hannibal. He has been careful to leave spaces between the different units of his legion. The elephants move into the spaces. And before long, the same thing happens in Zama as in Gaugamela: Hannibal turns pale, just as Darius turned pale. Both of them, a century apart, see that the elephants are overexcited, panicking. The sound of clarions, the press and shove of bodies around them are terrifying. They go into a rage, wheel around, lash out at random, return, and, without realizing, charge their own line. They can no longer retreat, they have moved too far into the enemy lines. Then the legions close around them, and in Zama, as in Gaugamela a century earlier, the great elephants of war become useless, massive beasts, and all of a sudden their trumpeting is the precise anthem of disaster.

"I absolutely will not move from here."

She tries one more time to persuade him. She tells him about the risk he is taking. The violence of these men who have death in their fingertips. She says he will be more useful out of harm's way, that UNESCO needs his knowledge about the site. She says that they can arrange everything to bring him to Europe. She personally will see to it, but Khaled al-Asaad says again, "I will not move."

There is a long silence.

And again she tries, with a soft voice, like a little girl pleading with her father: "Please, Monsieur Asaad . . . please."

Still he says nothing. Perhaps at this moment he is trying to gauge the consequences of his decision for himself and his family? Perhaps he can sense the future? When he starts to speak again, his voice is softer, too. He asks her not to be angry with him. "I'm an old man," he says. "My life is over. If I leave, everything will have been in vain. I can't, don't you see? I am taking precautions. My son Walid and I are trying to hide as many pieces as we can. I will keep watch over the site for as long as I live. Imagine Priam leaving Troy before the Achaeans get there . . . it's just not possible."

The conversation comes to an end. She knows she won't manage to persuade him to leave. With his son he will stay on, they will be the guardians of an empty temple, waiting for death. He will stay because to go anywhere else is to admit defeat. Does his age protect him from fear? Is it because his life is almost over that events can no longer affect him? She prepares to hang up, asking him to send her news, not to hesitate if he needs anything. He says yes, of course, thanks her. She knows he will do no such thing. Old Priam has closed the gate to the city of Ilion and he is waiting for the barbarians. He is doomed to watch as the world crumbles around him—there, from the place that is his: Tadmur, the pearl of the desert, the city of Queen Zenobia, whose sole guardian is an old man, eighty-three years of age, pacing to and fro between the columns and the ruins, keeping watch over the funerary towers and entrusting his fear to the evening wind.

In Zama as in Cannae, the first line holds. It retreats gradually, allowing the enemy to move in, and all Scipio has to do is what Hannibal himself did, as if in a sort of homage to the master, a vast circling movement that ensnares the Carthaginians. The Roman commander lowers his arm. This is the order to charge that Masinissa and his Numidan cavalry have been waiting for. They spur the flanks of their horses to make the enemy scream. Masinissa knows he has won, that henceforth he will reign over Numidia, from Siga to Cirta, that his rival, Syphax, will be swept aside. He knows he has just won his wager, and that he was right to change sides and betray Carthage, for very soon it will be nothing. The cavalry of the Massylii charge, and Hannibal knows that there is nothing left to do but leave Zama. He goes away, just as Darius went away, leaving the men behind him to finish dying. Some may yet fight, courageously. In the anonymity of the mêlée, there are surely still some warriors who will put their rage into the fight to repel the enemy, but to no avail. It will take time, a few hours or more, until the combatants' strength is depleted, until everyone sees that defeat is certain, until their bodies tremble with fatigue, and the most valiant among them resign themselves to placing one knee on the ground, and let their throats be cut.

"Burn everything! Burn everything!" At first the soldiers hesitate. They look at each other as if to see who will obey, but Sheridan exults. He points to the farm where they have just stopped, in the Shenandoah Valley, and he yells, "Burn it!" So they go ahead and do as he asks, somewhat shamefully. They will quickly get used to this and before long won't even think about it. All the farms they come upon along their way will suffer the same fate, and they will do as they are told without even noticing. "The Burning." This is what Grant asked Sheridan for: total war, make the villages weep. Before long they will lose all trace of their rather awkward hesitation, before long they won't even get off their horses. They will shoot them in the stomach without hesitating, those farmers who reach for a pitchfork to protect their harvest, and they'll put to the sword any wife who tries to intervene. Soon they will burn everything, systematically. For months. And Sheridan will no longer have to say it, to shout as he stands in his stirrups: "Burn everything!" They will have learned what to do. Grant often thinks he will have to seek forgiveness for these orders of his, because he knows the reality that hides behind them. And when he orders "the Burning" he can see the blackened farms and the crying children. So he turns in his mind to Julia, when he is drinking, unable to sleep, forgive me, Julia, women and children have been destroyed, he would like to say it, shout it: it is madness, what he is telling his men to do. "When I'm finished," Sheridan writes to him, "the valley will be unfit for man or beast," and that is what he does: the cattle are eviscerated, or, to go faster, burned alive in their barns, sometimes with the farmers, forgive me, Julia, don't ever look at me again with love. Victory is coming closer and the war is getting dirtier, more penetrating. It's been a long time since the men dreamt of nobility, they know that war is waged with a grimace and that they have lost their souls. This is what has been asked of them: to agree to bid themselves farewell and go into that vile place. And they do. Sheridan writes that the Shenandoah Valley is nothing but ashes, and Grant, upon reading him, feels no disgust; he has no right to. He is the one who required this of his men. If he must feel disgust, then let it be for himself, and that is what he does, but who can hear him? Julia goes on loving him, even as he is haunted by Sheridan's cries. "Burn! Burn everything!," and he has no right to consider this loathsome, for he is the one who is calling for it, and so he responds by ordering a salute of a thousand shots to be fired at Petersburg, in honor of those who have bled the earth of Shenandoah, "Burn . . . burn," and when he folds away his letter and looks up, he knows that a new manner of waging war has been born.

Defeated. He gazes out at the sea from the terraces of Carthage, the round harbor at his feet, with all its warships, and further out, the Mediterranean, this sea he never could master. Defeated. He says the word to himself again, and still he cannot quite believe it, but he saw the departure of the peace ship the Carthaginians had sent to Scipio, a boat covered in olive branches and white streamers, he saw it slowly, majestically pulling away from the harbor, heading west. He saw the faces of the Carthaginians in the street, and they know now that they are at the mercy of the victors. Is it really over? He had always thought that if he were to lose face to the Romans it would be at the cost of his life, like his brothers Mago and Hasdrubal. But here he is, alive, on the day Carthage must bow her head. The peace treaty has been signed. Everything is sealed. Carthage has handed over her war elephants. Carthage has agreed to have her fleet reduced to ten ships. Carthage has sent one hundred hostages to Rome, the sons of noble families, and they will be executed if she fails to honor her commitments. Carthage has agreed to pay the war indemnity, so that Rome will once again be prosperous. Rome will reign over this entire coast of the Mediterranean. From the terrace where he is standing he can hear the leader of the Punic fleet shouting his orders: "Burn!" and then, all at once, all the warships anchored off the harbor are in flames. Initially it is not visible. Perhaps he might have to repeat his order, "Burn!", but no, it is not necessary, the soldiers did obey him, under the gleeful gaze of the Roman envoys, who will later describe the scene in minute detail. He can hear it, the voice shouting, "Let it burn!", first smoke rises from the hulls, then the flames can be seen, "Let it burn!" It is as if the entire Mediterranean were on fire, there before his eyes, and along with it the memories of victory—Cannae, Trasimene, all pointless—burn the Barcids, who failed to bring the empire to her knees, burn Capua, cursed Capua, for opening her gates, and Masinissa the traitor with his entire Numidian cavalry, burn joy, something that will vanish from their lives, burn the sun, too, from tomorrow on freedom will be gone, and now it is the sails of the eighty war-ships that are burning, the wind carries the smell of fire and it is as if he had ashes in his mouth, burn, Rome has won and our elephants have died, an entire nation of soldiers watches in silence as the fleet burns, they have gathered from wherever they fell—the Iberian campaigns, the crossing of the Alps, the guerrilla warfare in the hills of Calabria—those who died in battle or those who died of thirst along the roads, burn, you are the army of the defeated and henceforth wherever you go you will bow your heads, burn, offshore the vessels are crack-ing, splitting, sinking: slowly, almost gently.

XI
CYRENAICA

Omar al-Dhour aged in only a few years. His face filled with lines, his eyes lost their sparkle. A deep fatigue burdens his gestures, even his smile. Assem remembers the first time they met. It was during the initial contacts that preceded the Franco-British attack in 2011. They fought side by side during the battle of Benghazi. Omar coordinated the redeployment of the city's defenders, while Assem provided information about ground strikes to the French fighter planes. How long ago it all seems . . . The elation over the fall of Gaddafi quickly subsided and gave way to a violent conflict over who would control the oil-producing zones. Islamic State arose. The country disintegrated, foundered in civil war. The fatigue is as legible on his friend's face as it is on the streets of Benghazi. Gone is all lightheartedness. Why has there never been a victory? Never a moment of full-hearted joy, followed by nothing more than quiet devotion to a peaceful life? Omar asks nothing of him. No questions regarding the reasons for his visit. He must have sensed that this is not an official mission. He takes Assem out onto the roof to the place where, in the days when they were defending Benghazi, they used to observe the city and the progression of the fighting, and he hands him a cigarette. Silence. That is what they need. No words can help them, not a single one. Then Omar tells him that tomorrow at five o'clock in the afternoon a man who has his complete trust will drive Assem to Sirte and even Tripoli if he can, as far as possible along the coastal road.

When did he cease to be the man who gave the speech at the League of Nations? His courtiers surround him, obsequiously. His courtiers smile at him and every day the palace is abuzz with hundreds of ridiculous little plots. They come to him to murmur of servile acts and ambition—some they warn against, others they seek to promote. He listens, never batting an eyelid. He never lets anything show. When did he stop being the brave man in Geneva, facing down the entire world, to become what he is today: a sad incarnation of privilege? He is the king of kings, the descendant of the Queen of Sheba. He does not have to be loved, he thinks, nor does he have to please. He just is, that is all. And they ask for nothing else, these men who conspire and whisper and walk on tiptoes, these men who scurry every morning to learn who is being denounced. So when did the common people begin to view things differently? Not his twenty-seven Rolls Royces, the luxury, the excess, not the panthers in their cages, the precious jewels; the hunger. Famine is widespread and he does not see it, or he thinks it will pass. The people are dying on their feet and no one seems to think it is urgent to try to save them.

When did they begin to win? The captain salutes him proudly as, with a slight, scarcely perceptible pressure of his thighs, he orders his horse to come to a halt: "Here they are, sir." He is proud of his catch, you can tell. He smiles and cannot help but add, "They're all along the roads. Lee can't hang onto his men." And the horse moves to one side to let the column of fugitives and deserters go by. They are not men anymore. They shuffle forward, their eyes wild, skeletal, weighing no more than half their original weight. Grant remembers the bodies in the trenches at Petersburg, when the town finally surrendered after nine months of siege. There were thirteen-year-old kids, barefoot, lying there in the mud. Shame on the Confederates who had armed them; shame on the soldiers who had killed them. They aren't men anymore. Neither those who are staggering there before him, who haven't eaten for days—just blades of grass, roots—nor he himself, standing here ramrod straight, upset by so much wretchedness, when it is he who decided to center the war on the supply routes, in order to starve the soldiers. He sees the young captain smiling at his side, happy with the day's catch, not at all bothered by the sight of a man with bleeding gums who has turned into a bag of bones. "War is hell," says his friend Sherman. Civilians must be punished and the enemy must be cut off from their bases. "I can make Georgia howl with pain," he wrote, and that is what he has done, destroying everything in his path. Here they are, the defeated, before his eyes, with their hollowed-out bodies, their white lips, their hallucinations of hunger. Should he be glad? Yes, because they are the emblem of his victory. Lee's army is melting away before his eyes. There cannot be more than thirty thousand left, and they are all starving. "War is cruel." He keeps thinking about Sherman, because only Sherman is lucid, only Sherman says things with all the brutality they contain. "The crueler the war, the sooner it will be over." The villages are burning. Men are dying of hunger on the road. Nothing can stop Sherman's advance. He goes through mud, forests. He is ransacking everything and the South is howling with pain. Should he, Grant, be glad? Just now he is thinking that victory is a test. He lets the ragged Confederates go by, and it seems to him that he is the one who has been humiliated—worse, he feels that this humiliation will never leave him, that he will have to learn to live with it, even when the shouts of victory sound out—for they will sound out—even then, it will be inside him, dull, penetrating, he won't be able to get away from it, and until his dying day it is something he will share with the enemy troops: this moment when, head bowed, man has sunk so low that he is no longer a man.

He will remember these moments for a long time, without knowing exactly whether he actually experienced them or whether they were some long dream inhabited by the sound of the sea and automatic rifle fire in the distance. He will remember this endless road for a long time, taking him from Benghazi to Tripoli, two days by car, two days of dust, across this battered country that smells of oil and fear. They drove for hours, trying to avoid junctions and checkpoints, hours of letting the countryside flash by, his face against the windowpane, looking for familiar signs of the place he had known a few years earlier. He remembers how the crowd shouted during the uprising, the groups of young men ready for anything, sometimes they had one rifle among four or five of them, and they swore not to give an inch to the troops that had remained loyal to Gaddafi. Now in the cities along the coast the streets are empty, and there is no jubilation. The young men climb into pickups in the morning and head off to terrorize the villages to the west. The country is falling apart. It is right that it should all end in Tripoli, because there is no doubt that everything will end. There will not be a third meeting. Job has summoned him one last time, and that will be the end.

Why does she keep thinking about him all the time? This man she will probably never see again, this man she spent only one night with? Why does her mind keep wheeling back to Zurich? His smell, the texture of his skin, it is all still inside her. She is thinking about him. And she could swear—she is deeply convinced—that wherever he might be, he is also thinking about her. Perhaps in the end that is why she got up and walked away from the man in the Hôtel Pullman. Not because she wanted to flee from his pathetic self-pity, as she initially believed she had done, not because it got her down, no, but because after Zurich she did not want to end up spending an awkward night of lovemaking—without conviction, pleasure more taken than given. Where is he right now? In what burning place on the planet?

The trip is long. And that is fine. He needs this time. They were not able to stop off at Leptis Magna as he had hoped: to see again those great Roman ruins above the sea, convinced of their eternity, defying the restlessness of humankind. He would have liked to stop there, because he senses it has something to do with Job. Once again he is on the road between Sirte and Misrata, this road where he met his shadow-line. Is it really a shadow-line? What Job felt in the helicopter coming back from Abbottabad, with bin Laden's body in a plastic tarp at his feet: this detachment from the world, this feeling that nothing can ever concern him after this: is that what he too felt on this road, three years ago, amid the crowd that sought to lynch the dictator?

Go, Hannibal, the night will protect you and the Romans will not find you, go, one after the other your horses become exhausted, white with foam, short of breath, but all the relays are safe, and there will always be one more horse to gallop anew and take you far from Carthage.

It could have gone on. A lifetime of reigning. Amid the immemorial pomp of the descendants of the tribe of Judah. It could have gone on for centuries. But they look strange, the authorities who are greeting him now on the tarmac of this airport in Brazil, and their faces are sinister. His plane has just landed for a State visit. He has flown over a part of the planet, carefree, thinking about the speeches he will give, and now the ambassador who has come to welcome him stands before him, his voice shaking: "Your Excellency . . . " He does not know how to say what he has come to tell him. He still cannot come to terms with the fact that he must inform his emperor that there has just been a coup d'état back home. The Negus freezes. He asks him to repeat what he has said, and to keep him informed of all the news they receive. The ambassador tells him what he knows: the two brothers Mengistu and Germame, whom he looked upon as sons, have seized power. They even entered the palace. Haile Selassie does not hesitate. He leaves again at once.

Go, Hannibal. Ten years ago Rome was victorious, Carthage bowed her head and has been paying her tribute to Rome ever since. And in spite of the conditions imposed by the Roman Senate, Carthage is doing well. When she offers to reimburse, forty years early, what she owes to Rome, the Senate trembles. They had not noticed that the vanquished city was so prosperous. Carthage is alive, Carthage is not dying. Hannibal is still there. Who is to say he might not have the means to go to war again? The Senate is finding it harder and harder to sleep. And this is vexing. They were the victors, after all. Why can they not enjoy the sleep of the just? Why are they afraid? Will it be enough for Hannibal, to spend his years overseeing the gilded mediocrity of his city, beneath the Roman yoke? Who can believe that? The senators know it, have felt it for a long time: nothing is over as long as Hannibal is alive. They were wrong to accept when Scipio interceded on the Barcid's behalf, requesting that he be allowed to live freely in his city. Scipio wanted to seem noble and magnanimous, but now the senators are trembling. The Barcid must die. Carthage is too wealthy. Hannibal must die because his life alone is a threat. His life alone is an encouragement to all those who hate Rome and are waiting for their chance. So they have decided he must die, and Hannibal knows it. In one night he leaves everything. He will never see Carthage again. He will never set foot upon the soil of Africa again. Go, Hannibal, from relay to relay, tonight as you are escaping the knife, hurry to the ship they have made ready for you, leave the coast as quickly as possible. Everything is beginning again, Hannibal. You may be alone on this small boat taking you to Cercina, but you have made Rome tremble. For the army of the dead arose with you to seek their revenge, and the imminent shock of empires arose with you— go, Hannibal, during this night of flight you will be reborn to yourself, the opponent, the ever possible course of action against the supremacy of Rome. It is all starting again. After the defeat at Zama, after ten years of silence paying the debts owed the victor, everything is beginning again, you know how to fight and you go in haste to the Orient, where you will find allies. The Seleucids are waiting for you. They want to overthrow the Roman empire, and with your name alone, with the blood you have caused to flow, you are enough to make that empire tremble.

The return flight is long, endless. He has had no news of his country. He does not know that to reassure the people his partisans have ordered one of his official cars to drive around the streets of Addis Ababa, and wherever it goes women ululate to salute the presence of the king of kings. He does not know that the two revolutionaries have occupied his palace and are holding eighteen people hostage. He knows he must get there as quickly as possible, that it is a matter of hours, that his presence in the city is vital, but the airplane can go no faster. And the second aircraft that is supposed to take him to the capital has a broken propeller. He decides to take off regardless, and he makes the trip tilted sideways in the sky, like his throne about to topple. He knows that from now on the joy that peace brings and the plenitude of power are things of the past. From now on there will be suspicion and solitude.

Outpourings of joy, everywhere. Custer raises his hat and his smile is triumphant. The men cheer him; he radiates pride.

Grant waits for them to give him the news. He doesn't like Custer, never has. He's always found him too pretentious, and unnecessarily cruel. How strange, in fact: there are, among the Confederate officers, men he respects infinitely more than some of those on his own side . . . At last they bring him the news: Custer and his men have seized a supply train and twenty-five cannon. The noose is tightening. Lee's column is being strangled. Grant shakes Custer's hand. This is good news, but that, too, is strange: men are going to starve to death and it is good news. Men who have already had nothing to eat for days, who are gaunt, who are deserting, staggering through fields, men who have become emaciated shadows, yet still they walk westward to try to escape from Grant and Sherman's armies: those men will have even less to eat. Men are going to die of hunger and Custer is raising his arms in victory. Grant hates him for doing that, but why shouldn't he? Why should he be sad in the midst of victory? Isn't this what they've been hoping for, for months, for years? The end is near. Perhaps this was the final blow. Yesterday he sent a letter to the Confederate leader to request his surrender. Lee hasn't replied. Now he knows that he will have to write another letter. What the last thirty thousand men of the Confederate column are going through is a nightmare. After the siege at Petersburg, after the great deadly attacks, the war looks like nothing so much now as a pursuit. The Confederate forces of Virginia are fleeing, they have nothing left. They cannot eat, they have no ammunition. They have been bled dry. That is the face of this war, the ugliest of all: a slow dying. There can be no more doubt: Lee has lost, and Grant wants there to be silence, deep silence so he can go back into his tent and write a new letter, but the men are shouting, tossing their caps into the air, singing and swearing to each other about how they will go and celebrate the victory in one of Washington's fifty brothels.

"Your Excellency . . . " He has been waiting for news but remains impassive. "The rebels have murdered the hostages." He remains upright, asks no questions. He is picturing the blood-soaked carpets in the palace, the moans of the victims, their entrails oozing, the disgusting stench of gunpowder and viscera. He knows he will be pitiless, he will punish the rebels, and that is what he does. When the soldiers find them, they spray Germame with bullets. Mengistu is wounded in the eye but still alive. They drag him off like an animal carcass. Haile Selassie has asked to see him. Just to stare at him calmly. He looks at him with scorn and orders for him to be hanged in the Mercato marketplace. Then for the remains of the conspirators to be put on display in Menelik Square, opposite Saint George's cathedral, where he himself was crowned. Flies will land on Mengistu's crushed eyebrow, on the gaping hole of dried blood, his tongue hanging out. Children will point at the strange, stiff, twisted bodies—how only a few days ago they caused the entire city to tremble. Everyone will see that the emperor has returned, and that he is strong. The people will know that those who oppose him end up with wretched, disjointed bodies that drip with blood. He knows that from now on everything will be distrust and whispering. Where is victory in a life of struggle, of coups d'état? When has he ever been victorious? Was it when he walked through the streets of Addis Ababa, upon his return, with Wingate by his side and the members of the Gideon Force behind them? That day when he was too hot, when he was eager to reach the palace so he could breathe at last? Was that the highest point in his life, a moment he should have managed to prolong somehow? Or was it earlier? His coronation? When he could still believe he would be the king of kings his whole life long? Now there is no longer any question of that. The war may have been long ago but from now on the threat to his throne will be everywhere. He looks at the flies on Mengistu's dead eyes and he knows that henceforth everything will be solitude and underhanded scheming.

Of course he has aged. Forty years of war have gone by. Forty years of being nothing but a warrior. A life of encampments, battlefields, rising at dawn, and long columns of horses. That is all he has ever known. He has never enjoyed his wife, his children, his country, the pleasures in life—or so rarely. He has devoted his entire existence to fighting Rome. And now, yet again. He is an old man now, but the soldiers in his presence still admire him. Hannibal. He has become that magical name, that *nom de guerre* that overthrows empires. Can the outcome still be reversed? He thinks it can. When he landed in Tyre, Antiochus received him with honors. Everything will change dramatically if the battle is won. Greece is not dead. She is playing her last card. She came for Hannibal because he is the man Rome fears most, the man who can help to overturn everything. A man of war, of experience. The Romans know that a threat is arising in the East. They know that they must crush this eastern front as quickly as possible. Now the two fleets are facing each other and everything will be decided. Hannibal watches as the ships are deployed. What is he thinking about just now? That he has never liked the sea? That Rome has always been able to rely on her fleet? That the world will tremble again, and that despite his age, he will once again be a master of war, no longer merely an opponent? What is he thinking? Perhaps deep down he knows he will not win . . . History does not give second chances. He is sixty years old now, and his war was lost when the gates of Capua were opened, or when the elephants at Zama went too far into the Roman lines. And what if today does not matter, in the end? What if the dead who fall today will fall in vain?

She leafs through the pages of a newspaper, in this little restaurant where she has come to eat by herself. The news is very distressing. The world is still reeling from the attack at the Bardo Museum in Tunisia. Many heads of state came to Tunis to march in protest. *"Ktema eis aei."* She thinks of how Thucydides used this expression to define the historian's process. Her professor, Ahmed al-Houry, drummed it into them, in Damascus, the year she spent at the Syrian university. To create "a possession for eternity." By describing the Peloponnesian wars, Thucydides hoped to leave humankind just such a possession: a definitive body of knowledge. Centuries have gone by. Historians have written, again and again, about every massacre, every genocide, every convulsion of History. "Never again." Every generation has uttered these words. Does History really serve no purpose? They had asked the old professor, she remembers it well, and Al-Houry had narrowed his eyes mischievously above his glasses, recovering for an instant his Lebanese lust for life. "I understand your dis-appointment," he said to his young students; she was one of them. "But don't reject Thucydides too quickly. Think about love . . . " And in the rows of the auditorium the young people leaned forward in surprise. "When you are about to declare your love, it is forever, isn't it? Never mind that there's a risk you might fall out of love, never mind your mothers and aunts and grandmothers who will tell you about the faithlessness of men and the erosion of time: in that moment when you are in love, it is forever, and it is the truth. So let us say, simply, that historians are young lovers . . . " And of course everyone in the auditorium had smiled, and the professor had savored the impact of his words before returning, gravely, to their study of *The History of the Peloponnesian War*. All her life she has been fighting, gathering artifacts, trying to rebuild the country's her-itage. She has always viewed museums as sanctuaries offered to the generations to come, containing the vestiges humanity has collected for eternity, relics that will not know the void. But are they really sanctuaries? She doesn't know anymore. She thinks again of old Professor Al-Khoury's mischievousness. Love. And then that face there before her: Assem. She knows she may never see him again, but in her innermost self she knows that she will possess that night in Zurich, for eternity . . .

In no time the battle begins to turn against them. Cursed ships . . . He will never manage to beat Rome on the sea. The Empire has fire ships. They are setting the sails of Antiochus's fleet alight, there are fires starting everywhere. The sea begins to glow. Hannibal clenches his teeth. Rome will win. Images are superimposed. He sees the Punic fleet burning in the harbor of Carthage, while Antiochus's ships crack apart and disintegrate. He is going to lose again. And the only question anyone will ask tonight, when they have withdrawn to Tyre, will be, should Antiochus hand him over to the Romans or not. Because they will ask, beyond a doubt. Will his ally hand him over for the sake of the treaty he'll negotiate, the peace deal he will wrest from them? That is the only question Hannibal takes with him as the ships turn around, abandoning the ones that have been hit, letting them burn, leaving the men to scream at the sea for rescue, to scream unto exhaustion, until they founder.

He has traveled all night from Misrata to Tripoli, prone in the back of the car so he won't be seen. When they reach the center of Tripoli the car leaves him on a street corner. He thanks the driver and heads into the city. He is alone now, walking quickly. No one seems to notice him. If they say anything, he'll pass himself off as a businessman or banker from Tunisia. He doesn't stop outside the façade of the former Radisson hotel, he has no need to catch his breath or assess the danger. He is in a hurry. So he steps on it. He goes into the hotel's spacious lounge where tired armchairs seem to be waiting for people who will come no more. The curtains have been drawn, to prevent shooting from the outside, no doubt . . . His eyes take a moment to adjust to the gloom. There is a man behind a counter that must have been the reception back in the days when the building was still used as a hotel, but he is absorbed in his newspaper and doesn't even look up. Assem walks ahead. On his right four men around a table are talking in low voices. Businessmen. A fifth one is standing slightly to one side with an automatic weapon slung over his shoulder. Assem turns to the left, toward the other lounge, and there he sees him, recognizes him immediately, he is alone and ensconced in an armchair, his eyes trying to penetrate the gloom, perhaps smiling, or grimacing, and the voice that greets him as soon as he appears is exactly the same as the voice in Beirut, as if it were merely the continuation of the same night: "I'm glad you found me, lieutenant . . . " And Assem has to confess that he is glad, too, and this unsettles him, because what can he be glad about just now?

XII
LIBYSSA

Grant has had a headache since dawn. If he had his druthers, he'd drink the whole bottle until he collapsed on his bunk and forgot the entire day. But he can't. He doesn't leave his tent. The light hurts his eyes. But they are calling for him. A voice full of urgency. "General Lee's reply, sir . . . " So he leaps to his feet. There's a man there, handing him an envelope. All the officers from his staff gather closely around the envoy and wait to hear the answer. He takes the envelope. Time stands still. Everything is slow. He hasn't opened the letter yet. He wonders if he has the strength. The officers are looking at him. Four years of conflict are weighing upon him. Dead men from all sides are craning their necks to read over his shoulder. So finally he opens it, and somehow finds the strength to read without his vision blurring: Lee is surrendering. He says as much, in just a few words. It's all over. Grant raises his head, impassive, hands the letter to those who are eager to read it. They take it from him—he doesn't even know who, exactly. He says nothing. Around him men are beginning to weep. Not to sing, or shout for joy: to weep over their own victory.

Antiochus did not betray him, but Hannibal has had to flee. From now on life will seem like little else: flight. He left Tyre for Crete, then Crete for the kingdom of Prusias. Every time, his life is in the hands of his host. Every time, the sovereign who takes him in must contend with Rome's displeasure. And he knows that someday he will be sold, or bartered in exchange for a peace treaty. He will be sacrificed as a pledge of goodwill, or surrendered as the final step in a long negotiation. What can he do about it? He is a fugitive along the eastern coast of the Mediterranean, from one country to the next, and until it ends his life will be nothing else.

There has been another coup d'état. Is it the same perpetrators? Have Mengistu and Germame come back from the dead to harass him again? No. They say it is something else this time. Not a man, but a sort of secret society: the Derg. He feels weary. So many years gone by . . . In his mind, the eras are beginning to overlap. The assaults on his throne are all superimposed. There have been so many conspiracies. Every two to four years. And now this one. They are firing at the palace and the people have not gone down into the street to protect him? Something has changed. Is he losing? He feels a sort of long-traveled fatigue take possession of him. It prevents him from leaping up, shouting orders, reacting vigorously. He senses that from now on his country looks on him with hatred, this man with his twenty-seven Rolls Royces, this man with his useless courtiers, this man with all his wealth in a country that is dying with its mouth open.

When Grant arrives at the McLean house in the village of Appomattox Court House, Lee is already there, wearing an impeccable uniform. Grant didn't bother to change. His uniform is caked with mud. It wasn't deliberate, to humiliate his adversary, he merely came as he was, covered in mud from the encampment. When he arrives, an air of solemnity overwhelms the place, crushing everyone there. In that moment Grant's face is strange. What it expresses, more than anything, is despondency. As if he were devastated by this victory. As if by putting an end to four years of bloodletting and carnage this moment were immersing him in the deepest sadness. Lee remains dignified, exemplary. To exchange a few words before the signing of the surrender, Grant reminds Lee that they have already met. It was during the Mexican campaign. He remembers well the aura around the Confederate general, already present in those days. He has evoked this memory to signal his respect, but that was in another life, and Lee doesn't remember. So many men have died since then. They shake hands. Lincoln has authorized Grant to give Lee generous conditions for the surrender. The Confederate soldiers will be disarmed and fed. The officers will be free to go. They must already look to reconciliation. When they leave the house in Appomattox the Union soldiers break into spontaneous shouts of joy, but Grant silences them with his hand. You do not celebrate victory when you have fought a civil war. Yesterday's enemy is tomorrow's neighbor. The ranks fall silent. And the men form a guard of honor for the Confederate delegation, who depart, jaws clenched, to inform their troops that they have lost the war, but there will be food to eat that night.

When he arrives in Libyssa, in Bithynia, Hannibal hears the news that Scipio has died. How strange . . . He has outlived the man who defeated him. Scipio was ten years his junior, but he has just died in Liternum, in his house overlooking the sea. Hannibal feels a peculiar sadness. As long as Scipio was alive he knew he could be sure nothing would happen to him. Scipio would not have wanted an unworthy fate for Hannibal. He had already protected him after the defeat at Zama, using his influence so that Hannibal could stay in Carthage. But now . . . When the time seems ripe nothing will stop them cutting his throat like a dog. He is no longer a warrior, for he has no more army. He is no longer a lord, because he is in exile, and he is not even an opponent because he no longer frightens anyone. He is a scarecrow, and someday they will kill him, waving their arms about to show how strong they are. He is a puppet, and his assassination will serve the other puppet who ordered it. Nothing more. That will be his life from now on, in this house by the sea, while he waits for the day of his death. And he no longer has any doubts that the world to which he belongs has begun to die.

What commanded respect yesterday is trampled underfoot today . . . Every morning the enemy comes to the door of his palace. Armed men in uniform climb the steps four at a time, with a list of names written on a scrap of paper. Every morning, the Derg comes and carries out its arrests: his ministers, his councilors, his courtiers, even his family. Bit by bit, day by day, he is being isolated, cut off. He says nothing, he looks at those who are led away, then he asks his valet to fetch him something to drink. He is less and less inclined to wander around the corridors. Everyone he meets wants something from him and he has nothing left to give. They beg him to react, to get organized or let his daughter do the maneuvering. He doesn't answer, he hurries out of the rooms when they approach him, leave me alone, he doesn't say it but his eyes express it whenever he runs into someone, leave me alone, he doesn't want anything anymore, he just asks his valet to come and help him get dressed at 4:45 every morning the way he always has, nothing else matters. Leave me alone, so what if there are arrests, and summary executions, and people strangled in barrack basements, provided they wake him up every day at 4:45. He no longer knows whether it is Mengistu or someone else who is attacking him, that strange society with a name but no leader . . . Leave me alone, he takes mincing steps like an old man in his embroidered dressing gown, sensing that his palace is humming with anxiety from the moment he gets up, because they all know that every day a delegation of military men with a list of names comes and knocks on his door, weapons in hand, and that every day men are disappearing, leave me alone, they tell him there is famine in the north of the country, they tell him there is corruption, the lists of names are getting longer and longer, and every day the palace is a little bit emptier, leave me alone, until the day he is the one the men in battle fatigues have come for.

Did he believe the blood would stop flowing with Lee's surrender? Did he believe he would luxuriate in peace one day, revert to his former innocence? There are too many corpses, and the dead are demanding their due. Grant saw the president this morning. He sat in on a cabinet meeting. Sat there listening to this man he admires, this man who has led them to victory, confident he is taking the right steps. Then he declined the invitation to the theater the president gave him, he took his leave and went back to Philadelphia. This evening they will bring him news. Initially he cannot understand why everyone is shouting, why people are weeping in the street, when it is already so late. The news travels by word of mouth, in the street, through the houses, throughout the country: Lincoln has just been shot, at Ford' Theatre, during the very performance to which Grant had been invited. Five days after the South surrendered, Lincoln is dead. The men killed in battle are here, ever more numerous, pressing with all their weight upon the world of the living.

His valet has come to warn him: the men from the Derg are waiting outside the door. He goes down from his room. The corridors seem so big, now that they are empty. He walks without haste. He goes through salons where pedestals have been overturned, smashed plates are on the floor. Why has no one picked them up? Disaster has been gnawing away at the palace. He goes slowly down the staircase. When at last he comes face-to-face with the military men—young men, with rough manners, speaking loudly to hide the fact that they are impressed, or not to show too much scorn—he hears the repeated order to go with them at once. He consents but demands that his valet be allowed to accompany him. He also asks to ride in one of his Rolls and not that horrible gray Volkswagen that is waiting for him at the entrance, between two military jeeps. The men in fatigues don't seem to understand. They categorically refuse, and drive him to the barracks. He says nothing more, does not protest. Now he knows the name of the leader of the insurrection: Mengistu Haile Mariam. He was right: perhaps it is, in a way, the spirit of the other Mengistu who has returned. It is all so confusing . . . It is said that this man's mother had been a servant at the royal palace. The common folk have rushed to the entrance to the palace to watch as he climbs into the Volkswagen: there is no cheering. In the old days, the people would shout with joy, wherever he went. Is this the irrefutable sign that everything is about to end, that the world he once knew, the world he reigned over, has been submerged?

Everyone around him is worried. It's not old age. It's not calumny, it's poverty. He is ruined. Julia is distraught. His friend Mark Twain has begged him to write his memoirs, and promises he'll get a good price for them. A life undone. He has been president. But will anyone remember? Two terms in office. Both tainted by corruption. Then he went around the world, slept in the finest hotels in Paris, London, New Delhi. He was greeted as a hero wherever he went and now he's ended up here, exhausted, with a blanket on his lap, with nothing to comfort him save the motion of the rocking chair, and his memories.

He gazes around his cell. This is where it all ends, in these four walls, in a soulless room, not really uncomfortable, but ugly. He won't move again, he'll stay here, in these barracks of the fourth division, the one that fomented the coup, the one that came and knocked on the door of the palace every day with a list of names, and that very evening led the dignitaries before the firing squad, within earshot of the palace. He is already familiar with exile, and flight, too; he has hidden in caves, walked through the night to escape his enemies in pursuit, but a tiny cell, never. He is learning. He has everything he needs. They feed him. They even took him to the Imperial Guard hospital to operate on his prostate. He does not think about anything, does not hope for any liberation. Oddly, he does not miss them, all those things he thought he could not do without—his valet, the grandeur of the court, his cook. He has been stripped of everything, does not own a single thing. There is no purpose to his days, not really. He talks to no one. He is just a body that goes on living, useless, isolated, invisible. And everything goes on, outside. The country is alive. Men go to work. He has departed from the world, he is undone, tiny, and no one is weeping for him.

Everyone is worried, but he is not. He'll write his memoirs. To leave something behind for his children, but deep down it hardly matters to him. Who can understand what his life was? He is naked and tired. He thinks endlessly about Lincoln, Lee, and Sherman. The only individuals he would willingly allow to pass judgment over him. They too have seen man in his nakedness. They too have ordered murder and been congratulated for it. They too have always known they had an army of the dead walking behind them.

Are they poisoning him? Yes, surely. But he goes on eating. What else can he do? He is convinced they are poisoning him because that is what he would do if he were in their shoes. A gradual death, one that can be passed off as a defeat of the body. Not a crime. Not an execution. That is what he did with Iyasu, Menelik's son and heir. He's not sorry he did. Iyasu was mad. Truly demented. The Italians wanted him to be king of kings and make him their puppet. He ordered him arrested and held prisoner in a hidden place deep in Harar. Then he poisoned him. Slowly. So that may well be what they are doing to him. But he couldn't care less.

One day—does the date have the slightest importance—death comes for him. It has the face of the son of one of the Libyssa fishermen. The young man comes in at a run, breathless, his face contorted by fear, and in an instant he knows that this is the last day of his life. "They've come . . . !" The boy says the words over and over, until he is gasping for breath. Hannibal tries to get him to speak. How many of them? Where are they? But the young man merely points behind him. And already he can hear the pounding on the door.

This is the time of disaster. Very often he feels cold. He can't smoke anymore. He is no longer allowed his beloved cigars, with their taste of encampments and horses. He lets his mind wander, constantly reenacting the battle. So many faces inhabit his mind, so many men who passed before him to the rhythm of armies or in long columns of prisoners, with the limping distress of the wounded or at a panicked run, so many men, at Lincoln's funeral, at the commemorations, a huge crowd filling his mind.

He senses instinctively that he won't have time to run away. And yet he has imagined this day. There are seven ways out of the house. He knew that sooner or later he would be sold to the Romans. But it all happens so quickly, he has no time to do anything. The door has been broken down. The assassins are coming. He has only a few moments left. In his ring there is poison: he opens it and greedily swallows the contents.

He is learning to live in a room he cannot leave, preserving his old man's impassivity, as if everything had abandoned him long ago—fear, joy, feelings of ambition or desires for revenge, as if there were nothing left but a dried-up husk of a man who has agreed to be rolled between the hands of History. Nothing matters to him. He is just that man, there, in a cell, a stone's throw from the palace where he used to reign. History has decided it will end like this, and he is empty, has been drained of all the tumult that followed him everywhere during his lifetime, as if the only gift History could give him would be silence, the great, appeasing silence that comes before death.

It is the time of disaster now and that is fine. He would blush if he died in glory. The fact that he is ruined and suffering from the cold doesn't matter. He lost the words with which to complain long ago, and he is slowly getting used to the idea of ending up on his patio, in those gentle hours when the light fades, before the damp takes hold of him. Men always end their lives in defeat. He takes with him his memories of fever, his nights of drink, his exhaustion from the war, he takes with him everything he has been and dies without regret because the rest is nothing.

He reaches for a sword, because he would like to die with his weapon in his hand and keep his enemies at bay long enough for the poison to take effect, but the weapon seems incredibly heavy and he cannot stop it from falling to the floor with a dull metallic clang. His head is spinning. The Roman soldiers enter the room, their faces heavy, their hands thick. How many are there? He's not sure he'll manage to count them. His vision blurs. A white foam oozes from his lips. He can just make out the surprise on his assailants' faces before he falls to the floor: that surprise is a victory he holds close in his mind.

And then one day Mengistu Haile Mariam comes in to see him in his cell. He has come to kill him. He can no longer wait for old age or poison to finish him off, it's too slow. Do they speak? What could they say to each other? Haile Selassie knows what his executioner has come for. He doesn't want to plead. He doesn't move. He remains impassive, the way he always has. He is nothing but a dried-up little man who will not take long to die. Mengistu comes closer, he will suffocate him between two mattresses. It will take only a few seconds, a few minutes at the most . . . He will squeeze hard, using all his weight, and a world will disappear. They do not speak. There is nothing to say. One man has come to kill the other. That's all. The day outside is vast, but Haile Selassie will not see it. Mengistu comes even closer, leans over the bed, and already there is not enough air.

How long does he lie there on the floor, dying, yet conscious? How long before one of the killers, perhaps, annoyed that he has not been able to fulfill his mission as planned, stabs him with his own sword or cuts off his head? How long before he slips away? He reflects on his life—a long warrior's gallop across a blazing land—and thinks again of the victory he is taking with him, in spite of death, the victory of having become a name his enemies cannot capture: "Hannibal," and he smiles.

It's all over.

Sheridan. Grant. Sherman. Lee. A generation of heroes, of butchers. Who might grieve when they are gone? There can be no sadness. More like relief. Too much blood. The blood spilled, which they walked in, and the blood that spread into the earth, nourishing the trees on the battlefield.

They have buried each other. The day of Sherman's funeral the Confederate general Johnston, his enemy, carried his coffin. It was raining and they told him to put on his hat. He refused, saying that would be unworthy, and that if Sherman were carrying *his* coffin, he would certainly not put his hat on . . . Johnston was obstinate. He ended up catching pneumonia and died of it several weeks later. They are bound by blood, and die together.

There are the remains. The ones that are hidden, and the ones that are glorified. The nation built a huge mausoleum for Grant, and it must seem quite empty to his poor skeleton. Perhaps he would have preferred a tree on the battlefield at Shiloh, but heroes are doomed to marble . . .

For the bodies of the defeated, there is still hatred.

The secretary of war, Edwin Stanton, asked the quartermaster general to deal with it: find a place for all the bodies left by this huge fratricidal butchery. And Montgomery Meigs decided on Arlington, General Lee's former estate. They built the nation's military cemetery in the defeated man's garden.

Hannibal's body is hidden, buried in secret. It is hurriedly spirited away because, even lifeless, he still causes Rome to tremble.

One day at the bottom of a hole in the barracks basement in Addis Ababa they will find the Negus's remains. A ceremony will be held at Saint George's cathedral so that his bones, tarnished by thirty years of obscurity, can become relics, and so that the king of kings, the lion of the tribe of Judah, may rest in peace.

But can they, all these men, really rest in peace?

XIII
ALEXANDRIA

She is in Alexandria, in the Mediterranean night, on that shore where the air is humid and at sunset the swallows make a deafening racket. She is there while he is in Tripoli, almost next door, but they don't know it. She cannot sleep. Her room has a little balcony overlooking the sea and she has gone to sit out there. Her legs on the parapet, her skirt pulled up to catch a bit of cool breeze, she thinks about Marwan. The gentle night air enfolds her. She remembers the last time they met. She saw him again after they split up. Just once. He was the one who called her, when he knew she would be passing through Cairo. His voice over the telephone had changed, grown older. He asked her if they could meet at the Café Riche at six in the evening. She said yes. In the hours leading up to their appointment she wondered what he might possibly want from her. There had been an urgency in his tone. She got to the café early. She sat down at a little table that faced the entrance and ordered a tea. Oddly, the café was rather empty. And then he appeared in the doorway, and she almost put her hand up to her lips. He had lost weight, and he walked like an old man. It was obvious that this was the first time he had been out in a long time. He was wearing a good suit but it hung loose on his body and he looked like a tired marionette. What sort of pretext had he used to leave the house to come and meet her? He smiled when he saw her. She didn't know whether she should stand up and kiss him on the cheek. He swept away her hesitation with a wave of his hand that meant she shouldn't get up, then he collapsed on his chair like an exhausted swimmer who has finally made it to shore. He was short of breath. His face was emaciated. The waiter told him it was a pleasure to see him again, bowing and scraping and calling him sir, before he went off to prepare a second cup of tea. They didn't talk about themselves, about their affair or the breakup. They didn't talk about the illness that had depleted him and would soon ensure there was nothing left of him in his huge baggy suit but bones. That was not why he was here, she had sensed that instantly. Once the second cup of tea was brought and they would no longer be disturbed he reached in his bag for an object wrapped in tissue paper which he placed on the table. "I'm going to tell you a story," he said. "Don't ask me anything, don't say anything. And in the end, you can take this package, or leave it." And so, in the rather sleepy setting of the Café Riche, he began telling his story. Nothing could make him lose focus, neither the shuffling steps of the waiters nor the occasional group of students bursting in, giddy and excited, as if they had arrived at a place where the future of tomorrow's world would be decided; with Mariam they seemed to be cut off from the rest of the world. He talked about Mariette Pasha. He invoked the feverish hours of the excavation of the Serapeum, when modern archeology was in its infancy. He spoke about the fierce competition among the various European nations in Egypt in those days. Both Lepsius, the great German archeologist, and Mariette knew that supremacy would fall to whoever managed to acquire the most, and fastest. And then there was Salomon Fernandez, the so-called antique dealer who pillaged the sites. Ever since the Napoleonic campaign Egypt had been an open air antiques market. "Just imagine," said Marwan with a sort of rediscovered jubilation, "what they went through, those men. Between plunderers and archeologists . . . " And he explained how you had to be clever in order to obtain a firman. That sometimes the right to dig was granted in the most random of ways. That Mariette, while waiting for his firman, had had to interrupt his excavation. "And so," said Marwan, "do you know what he did? An archeologist. Like you or me, who knows he's in the right place, that everything he has been looking for for months, or years, is there beneath his feet, but he can't dig because he hasn't got the official paper with the stamp, because he hasn't knocked at the right doors or hasn't oiled the right palms, so what does he do?" He went on to list the ways Mariette Pasha got around the absence of a firman: he would dig at night, once the supervisors sent by the powers that be had gone home for the night, by torchlight, and with a smaller team. Then smuggling the artifacts out with the help of foreign visitors. To avoid detection by the authorities, every French visitor would leave with a statue or a jewel hidden underneath the ladies' shawls or in their handbags. Wasn't that plundering, too? The sort of tricks pirates got up to? And yet Mariette created archeology and chose Egypt; he settled in Bulaq, founded a museum there. He is still buried there, outside the museum he gave to Egypt and which was one way to stop the artifacts being sent to the Louvre. She listened, wondering why Marwan was telling her all this, but taking the time to gaze at his eyes, which had lost none of their sparkle. "And then one day Mariette went to see Paul-Émile Botta in Paris. I don't know where they met. Maybe at Botta's house. Mariette was young and probably nervous and intimidated. There before him was the consul of Mosul, of Jerusalem, of Tripoli. And above all there before him was the man who had discovered the giants of Khorsabad. I don't know when he set his artifact down in front of Botta, or what he said. I imagine he talked about how important it was not to forget that we are tomb robbers. That the pharaohs shut themselves away in their tombs for all eternity, and that for us to open those tombs, to break and enter, even in the name of History, is still nothing more than some pirate incursion. We mustn't forget this. We create a science, we are rigorous, we study at libraries, we talk about heritage, and History, and the memory of civilizations, but we shouldn't keep silent about this thing: the pleasure we get from breaking and entering. The skeletons and mummies, the funerary objects—we're stealing them from the void. We open rooms that ought to stay closed. Yesterday it was with dynamite, today it is with infinite precaution, but woe to anyone who forgets that the basic gesture remains the same. That is what Mariette must have said to Botta, then he handed him the object he had brought for him. Not as booty. Not like the empress who a few years later would ask him for Queen Ahhotep's jewels—which he refused to give her, as it happens, he was incensed by such an obscene demand—no, he handed the artifact to Botta as a pact. They were both men who had been on digs, mounted expeditions, headed teams, and they needed to share a stolen object that would be handed down from generation to generation so that no one would ever forget that archeology is only a step away from pillaging. But Botta looked at him, dumbfounded, his cheeks red. He frowned, stammered, protested. How dare you, young man . . . or something like that. Do you take me for a pillager? I have worked for France. For humanity. He tossed all these grandiose words in Mariette's face like so many slaps on the cheeks of a fifteen-year-old shoplifter. It was a disgrace. And all this . . . because he didn't get it, didn't know that the man there before him didn't need any lessons in ethics. That he would go on to give far more to Egypt than anyone else in that era. And Mariette went away again, crestfallen, wondering what had come over him, even worried that the consul might denounce him. Time went by, but the idea remained: a stolen artifact so that we may never forget that archeologists are tomb robbers. And when the young Maspero came into his life, just before his wife and daughter died and he buried them in the cemetery in Old Cairo, he identified him as his worthy successor. Maspero was brilliant, elegant, cultured. Mariette had the feeling that Maspero's generation would be more methodical than his own, more scientific, and then he thought again about the artifact, because it would perhaps be even more crucial for these men of the scientific era not to forget the notion of breaking and entering. So he handed his artifact to the young man, who must initially have been surprised, even stunned, and a little bit ashamed because he had probably never stolen a thing in his life, but Maspero was smart, so he accepted it."

With her feet on the railing of the balcony, she recalls Marwan's story. That final meeting at the Café Riche. He eventually fell silent. And his hand nudged the package there in front of him. "I've kept it my entire life. Not as a thief . . . Because it was my duty. I always knew that I would give it to you." And those were the last words she heard from his lips. After that he was silent, letting her take her time to put her hand on the object and slowly remove the tissue paper. She opened her mouth wide when the statue of the god Bes appeared before her. In black stone, as big as her palm. The dwarf god with long arms and short stocky legs. The face of a lion and a thick beard. The god who performs his grotesque, grimacing dance to chase away the forces of evil, to protect men from nightmares and sexual malfunction. The god Bes who is placed under the head of the dying at the moment of their death in order to look after them in the hereafter. The ugly, belching hairy dwarf with his thick eyebrows. She takes him in her hand, oblivious as to whether anyone in the café is looking at her or not, whether anyone around them is wondering what on earth that thing is . . . She accepts, and Marwan smiles. She remembers that moment: when Marwan smiled. He got up, said nothing more. Nothing. Not even "goodbye"— because the right word would have been "farewell"—let alone "see you soon," because that would have been a lie. He paid and left, and she let him go off with that cane she had never seen him with before, walking like a mountain that is crumbling, she let him go to his submersion and she clutched the dwarf god tightly. She remembers this. And tonight, on the terrace in Alexandria, she thinks again of Marwan with the feeling that for the first time she is no longer a mistress who has lost her lover. She has learned to be without him. She thinks again of the god Bes, the feel of stone in her hand. A statue that was buried in the earth thousands of years ago, until Mariette Pasha held it, then Maspero, then others, a long chain of archeologists who agreed, on taking it, to acknowledge the shadow side of their profession. And Botta should have taken it. If he had known that two hundred and nine crates filled with the ancient artifacts exhumed from the site he had discovered were about to sink to the bottom of the Tigris, he would have taken it. She thinks of this long chain of men and women leading down to her and to the man she gave the statue to—possibly the first not to be an archeologist. And so? What does she know? The Bes statue has been restored to life, shunted from one country to the next, one convulsion to the next. Some people died, others wanted to get rid of it, but until it came to her the artifact was always passed on. She wonders how much of her gesture Assem will understand, what he will make of the object, what he will do with it. She thinks about him. And it's strange, but she thinks about him the way she would think about a lover. Will they ever meet again? Their time together seems to have expanded inside her since they met. He has begun to take up room. She thinks about him, during this night that has brought them together on this same shore of the Mediterranean, wrapped in the same thick, humid heat that is causing the palm leaves to wilt from Alexandra to Tripoli, and she hopes that the dwarf god is watching over him wherever he might be, banishing with his grimacing face the nightmares that hover over human beings.

XIV
TRIPOLI

He is sitting across from Job. The American lets him get settled, looking at him calmly, then with a strange smile he asks, "Why did you come?"

He is not sure he knows but he answers anyway.

"So we can finish our conversation."

Job smiles.

"You're better than they are, lieutenant . . . " And he pours a drink. Then he says, playfully, "You're right. You're here so that there can be an ending. And that's good. That's what I hoped."

And before Assem can speak again, he continues: "It is defeat that unites us, lieutenant . . . "

And now Assem feels what he had felt in Beirut: that all at once, through the power of words, time has expanded.

Job's eyes are shining in the gloom of the salon. There is the sporadic sound of automatic weapon fire in the distance. He isn't startled, but for a split second a shadow of anxiety passes over his face. Defeat . . . Assem knows that Job is telling the truth. He know that this is what they have shared all along: the deep conviction that they have been defeated. And it's no longer a matter of success versus failure. True, deep defeat, the defeat that one fine day humans feel inside like a force weighing upon them, will make them less quick, less innocent; there is the defeat of the body, thickening, swelling, becoming short-winded, and of eyes that wish they had not seen so much. The deep, private defeat, in the face of this thing that is drawing closer, from which no one can escape, and which is called submersion.

234 · LAURENT GAUDÉ

"What are the causes we have fought for, lieutenant?" Job asks again, seeming more and more agitated. Assem doesn't know how to answer his question. So he asks one himself.

"What," he says bluntly to the American, "are you going to do now?"

The other man doesn't flinch, looks at him forcefully and says:

"The battles we were asked to win—we've won them, but you and I both know that we have been defeated, we can feel it inside, something has gone too far, or has lost its meaning . . . Don't you think so, lieutenant?"

Assem remembers that day, always the same one, on the road to Sirte, when he was among the crowd of Libyan opponents, that baking day with Gaddafi's disarticulated body and the sound of gunfire in the damp sky. Part of him was left behind there, and Job may well be right . . .

"Now I'm going to tell you what we're going to do," says Job, with greater assurance and a strange smile. "I'm going to tell you what I am. Really. Unmasked. And when I'm done, it'll be up to you to judge. All right? When I say judge, I mean it will be up to you to tell me whether I should live or die."

There is not a sound in the hotel lobby, only his voice, thick, stubborn, which seems to have taken possession of the space and reigns over the sofas and armchairs like a sovereign in his realm, as he continues.

"That is why they sent you, isn't it? To find out whether I should live or die? I'm not asking you anything more than what they asked you. Except that they want to know whether I represent a risk for the United States, or something like that . . . Forget them. Between you and me it's different."

Assem answers rather quickly, as if he wants to avoid venturing into territory where he senses he might get lost.

"You know they're going to do all they can to neutralize you?"

Job takes his time, looks at him with a sort of kindliness in his eyes and says, "We're beyond that."

Assem doesn't know what to say. The conversation is taking an unpredictable turn. He would like to get up and leave.

"I don't understand," he stammers.

"Yes you do, you understand perfectly," answers Job, with a hard gaze. "And you know that this is how it will end. If you think I have to live, I will go away and they will never find me. But I want to hear it coming from your mouth. We're done with obeying, you and me. What exists between us now is loyalty."

Assem would like to say no, to find the words to make him see reason, but he doesn't move, doesn't speak, seems to consent, and so Job continues: "I'm going to tell you what happened in Kalafgan."

There is no one left around them. The businessmen already got up and left a long while ago. The glasses are still on the table and everything seems so still, so frozen, that it is hard to guess how long they will stay there. They are alone in the building. The humid night comes through the half-open windows only when a puff of wind has enough strength to lift one of the heavy taffeta curtains—vestiges of a time when the place was awash with money.

"Did you know that in Antiquity there were priests who believed you could know the will of the gods by studying the way children moved around the playground? When they play, their shouts and moves, the gestures they make, the fights they get into, their games, it all makes sense."

"Why are you telling me this?" asks Assem.

"Because that is what I did," continues Job, his voice hard. "In Afghanistan, in Kalafgan, I did that. I watched a schoolyard full of children. How they came and went. And shouted. Their footprints in the dusty ground. And the gods spoke to me. It was beautiful. The light of the sky. Their chiming voices. I swear. It was beautiful. But do you know what I heard? 'Destruction.' That was the word the gods murmured in my ear. Right there, with the kids coming and going: 'Destruction.'

I felt it as if the word were written on the air, as if the children themselves had asked for it. I had to kill something, absolutely, as quickly as possible. So I did. The gods don't lie, do they. I obeyed them. I sent the coordinates of the madrasa to Creech Air Force Base in Nevada and a missile took off from far away and came to land there before me, and the will of the gods was done. Destruction. The children were no more. I did that and I stayed to the end so I could walk through the schoolyard once the fire had died down and I could listen to the silence, but there wasn't any silence, just the villagers screaming, hands grabbing me, hatred everywhere, mine, theirs, I could understand their insults, and I shared them, and I could have hit them the way they hit me, it hardly matters, it was hitting that was needed just then, one way or the other, so that it would all be over, that's what the gods had asked for, for stones to be thrown, blows to be delivered, I thought it would end there but they rescued me. That was the expression they used. I should have jumped out of the helicopter. I thought about it: jump, and die torn to pieces in the dry stones of Kalafgan, but there were no gods to tell me to do that. They had fallen silent."

Assem says nothing. He is stunned by what he has just heard. Job takes his time. Maybe he's thinking about Jasper Kopp. He has just let out the secret Kopp had taken to his grave, and Kopp, back there, should be able at last to cry out from beyond death, in his relief that someone knows what he did. Then suddenly Job starts speaking again.

"So, lieutenant. Should I die?"

Assem feels hot, unwell. He doesn't want to hear this question and all that it implies.

"Let me go," he murmurs. And so that Job won't start talking again, he repeats it, louder, "Let me go." He is about to get up but Job is quicker. Brusquely, he pulls his hand out from under the table and shouts, "You're not going anywhere, lieutenant. You promised. Loyalty. Remember? Now you have to answer me."

And in his hand he is holding a grenade.

"What are you doing?" says Assem.

"Have you decided?"

Before Assem has any time to react, he hears a noise: Job has just removed the pin from the grenade. He is holding it close to him now. At any moment he can let go of the lever and everything will blow: the armchair, the table, Assem . . . They can die together. It depends on Job. If he releases the pressure of his finger, it will all end here. But he doesn't, he goes on sitting there, his hand tight around the grenade, staring at Assem.

"Should I live?" he asks.

Assem says nothing. He has no more words.

"Look at me!" screams Job. His eyes are feverish. Assem looks up and stares him right in the eyes. "Say something! Or can't you? Answer, lieutenant!"

And Assem, barely audible as he exhales, lets out one word, "Die . . . ," and just as he hears it, strangely, Job's face lights up, not despondent like that of a prisoner who has just been given his sentence, but relieved, as if he had been waiting so long for that word, as if it was the finest gift anyone could give him, and then he says, with a grateful smile, an almost handsome smile despite the feverishness in his eyes:

"Death rather than my carcass . . . That's good. Thank you. All is well."

Assem slowly gets to his feet. He senses that Job will let him go, that he is no longer with him, doesn't even seem to see Assem anymore. His hand is still clutching the grenade, his face turned slightly upward, he's communing with invisible forces, light-years away from the city around him, he's staring down the centuries. Maybe he is summoning the ghosts of the children and of Jasper Kopp, unless he is remembering the night at Abbottabad, the sound of the helicopter during the flight back, with that body at his feet, or the schoolyard in Kalafgan beneath the Afghan sky, and the oracles that said nothing but "destruction" . . . Assem moves backward one step at a time, slowly, then goes out, leaving Job behind him without another word, without another look. They are too far apart now. He does not turn around. The air in the street feels good. A few cars in the distance drive quickly along the seafront. He crosses the street, knows that everything is coming to an end there in that room he has just left. Job must have stayed in exactly the same position he'd been in, perhaps speaking to his ghosts, or cursing his enemies . . . Until the explosion rips through the silence, muffled by the thick walls of the Radisson. He knows that throughout the neighborhood men and women will have woken with a start, wondering what has just happened. He knows that someone will eventually go to see but no one will find a thing, because all there is up there are bits of charred body parts and a smile floating through eternity.

XV
CANNE DELLA BATTAGLIA

Everything in the main hall of the museum is quiet, and yet the world is on fire. Palmyra has fallen. They have murdered Khaled al-Asaad. She just found out. She is walking through this room in the Bardo where she has been attending a conference on heritage conservation. A few months ago there were people here who were running, screaming, bleeding . . . They have come here, symbolically, to lend their support, reassert their values. They spoke, the audience applauded, and then one of her colleagues leaned over to her and murmured: "They've beheaded Khaled al-Asaad," showing her his telephone with the news brief from one of the news channels. She stood up, unsteadily. She left the gallery. She wanted to be alone with the artifacts. She wandered slowly through the huge museum, its name now marked with blood, and stopped only when she had the red terra-cotta mask in front of her, with its twisted nose, grimacing mouth, and those two dark holes for eyes. Who is he laughing at? Is it her? Their impotence in the face of barbarity? Her illness? Kind Dr. Hallouche's comforting words as he looked at the results of the test, the way a father would look at his off-spring's report cards? No. The mask is looking further: at the men rushing past his eyes, at the men and women going back and forth in front of this display case. The day of the attack the mask saw people panicking in this museum that had become a trap. He heard the shots, the screams. Maybe he saw the traces of blood along the walls . . . And he grimaces at the sight of humanity's self-slaughter. Does he grimace from disgust or simply to ape the madness of men? The entrances to these buildings will soon be better guarded than embassies or barracks. The murderers are the same men who attacked the colossuses at the museum in Mosul with their angle grinders, the same men who occupied the Zenobia Hotel in Palmyra, looking at the ancient relics with a vulture's appetite, the same men who want to make women forget how to read, who burn the past and topple columns at timeless sites. She stays in the room looking at the red mask for a long time, until she concludes that he hasn't been looking at anything. No. The holes in the place of eyes are there so that you can enter into him, so that you can be snatched away by the centuries. And the open mouth, too. So for the space of a few minutes she immerses herself in the mask, into a space where there is no one around her, she is far away from everything, from Dr. Hallouche telling her that the results are encouraging, from the other participants at the conference who are scattering in little groups through the huge rooms of this museum that was built as a palace for mosaics but has ended up a tomb, far from her colleagues walking through the rooms trying to be as quiet as possible, intimidated by the pervasive sensation of death. She leaves all that and, paradoxically, she feels strong. Here, facing the mask, for the first time in weeks, she feels determined. The struggle will continue. In spite of the fatigue her treatment will cause her, she will go on working, coming and going between Paris and Baghdad, from rich, potbellied Europe—Geneva, Zurich, London—to these ever-turbulent lands, but she still has the strength, so she will do it. She will hunt down the plundered artifacts, will defend the museums they want to burn. She places her hand on the glass opposite the mask and it is like a promise. The words she said during the conference that has just ended, about the battle against obscurantism and how they cannot afford to lose it, must never lose it: that is something she believes in. And the death of Khaled al-Asaad does not cancel out her words. Blood will flow again. Marvels from ancient times will be sold on the black market or destroyed, men and women will be murdered, but there can be no defeat. Because that would mean accepting a loss of our identity, that would mean making us forget how to live. We have been reading poetry for too long, we have been admiring mosaics for too long to give all that up. From Alexandria to Baghdad. From Tunis to Palmyra, she will carry on until exhaustion, but that does not matter, because there can be no defeat.

He is driving southward. The August heat causes the air to vibrate. On his left is the Adriatic coast. Before he reaches Barletta he leaves the main road and heads inland. Initially he doesn't see it, then at last there is a little sign indicating the presence of a river: the Olfanto. At this time of year the riverbed is dry and it seems so narrow, so insignificant. No more than a ravine full of weeds. By the side of the road, after a bend, there are prostitutes standing in the shade of an unfinished bridge. Fifteen-year-old kids. They must be Romanian or Albanian. With the bodies of children, almost no breasts, but already their poses are lascivious. He has time to look at them as he drives by. The road is narrow. They call out to him, make gestures that try to be enticing but are simply terribly sad. They are in the middle of nowhere, in this sunstruck countryside, along a little road with no trucks going by. What are they doing there, beneath that dirty bridge, lurking like alley cats? He drives on. It is all depressing, but when seen as a whole, the silence of the place lends it a majestic beauty. And what if they were part of that beauty? Those little girls with their tainted bodies, there in the middle of nowhere. Everything is where it belongs. Ugliness and beauty. Sacrifice of innocence and majesty of nature, nature that keeps silent because it is too hot, but it is biding its time, waiting for the day to fade or the wind to rise, waiting to make noise and come to life again.

She has managed to delay her flight for two days. She wants to stay here in Tunis, on this avenue Bourguiba, which the barbarians look upon with hatred because of its freedom, because women walk down it and look straight ahead, proud they took part in the fall of the dictator. She wants to stay in Tunis because there is a headiness in the air. Like in Erbil. Who knows what these places will be like in a year or two? Who knows whether this is the beginning of a new era, vast and full of possibility, or just a parenthesis that will soon be closed? At Bab El Bhar she hails a taxi and has it take her to Sidi Bou Said. She wants to drive along the coast, let her gaze linger on the Carthaginian sites. She asks the taxi to go by the Punic port, down the street where there is the entrance to the children's cemetery. He tries to explain to her that it will make the trip longer, but she insists, she doesn't want to stop, or get out of the car, just drive by and see for herself that everything is there, immutable, and that nothing trembles, because these places have lived through the fall of civilizations and oblivion and the solitude of time, but are still there, in spite of everything, watching us.

He eventually reaches his destination and parks the car outside the entrance to the site. There is no one around. It occurs to him that it might even be closed. At this time of day, in the middle of August, when it is so hot . . . And yet it isn't closed. The door is unlocked and a little man is sitting in the ticket office. He doesn't seem surprised to see a visitor, nor does he ask any questions, whereas Assem muses that if he were in the man's shoes he would be curious to find out what brings people here. It is very quiet. He doesn't spend any time in the building but heads immediately up the hill. Canne della

Battaglia. That is what they call the place nowadays. From up here he can see the sea. Behind him the sun is setting. A gentle wind blows in from the sea and makes a faint whisper in the pine trees. There is not a soul around. An ancient silence. To his left he has a perfect view of the Gargano Promontory in the distance. Below him, down the hill to the sea, there are pine trees and oleander, and always this silence. Vineyards now cover the area where the battlefield was. What sort of wine do they produce? Over the years the roots must have worked their way through fragments of weapons, of skeletons. He can hear the peaceful cooing of turtledoves in the distance. It all radiates a feeling of peace. The road, the towns, the heat of the crowd are all far away. And yet he is standing on a graveyard. Canne della Battaglia. It was here that Hannibal defeated the Roman army. Here that in the space of a few hours forty-five thousand Romans were slain. The plain there below him, so lovely, so gentle, stank of viscera for a very long time. He tries to imagine it: forty-five thousand mutilated, dying men, still moving slightly, trying in vain to drag themselves somewhere or begging for someone to come and help. Perhaps this is why the place seems so silent: it is the silence of the grave. How can the site of one of the greatest bloodbaths in human history be magnificent? He feels the warm wind from the sea fill him. The summer light settles gracefully on the distant hills. Job is back there, dead by his own hand as he released the grenade, blown to bits by the explosion, beheaded by his own will. It is all over now. The air is soft. So he leans down to the ground. There. At the top of the hill. And he begins to dig a hole at his feet, slowly, without hurrying.

They reach the very top of the village of Sidi Bou Said. The taxi driver stops by the lighthouse. She pays him, gets out, and walks to the little marine cemetery that sits imposingly at the top of the hill. There is an expansive view over the sea. She perches on the little wall and gazes out at the immensity. She is very close to him. In the same stillness of the world, she is withdrawing, like him, to let the silence of the hills enter her; nothing else matters. She has come here to pay tribute to Khaled al-Asaad. The old man was tortured for days. The barbarians wanted to know where the treasure of Palmyra was hidden. He resisted, scorned them until the end. They took a knife and beheaded him in the very place that had been his entire life. And then they suspended his body on a cable from a crane, with his head propped on the ground by his feet. Old Priam, violated even in death. Not for him the shade of the tower tombs or the soft earth of Tadmur. He is floating, heavy and ugly, in the hot desert air, like a carcass at the slaughterhouse. Tomorrow they will raze Palmyra. Tomorrow they will dynamite the ancient city's temple of Bel, the tower tombs, and the avenue of columns. Nothing can stop them. She wants to think about him. So she gets up, with the cemetery's tombs behind her, and she closes her eyes as she turns toward the sea. She lets the wind fill her. She thinks of Khaled al-Asaad and murmurs an old prayer in Aramaic. So that Antiquity will be there, by her side. The graves of the marine cemetery look out at the horizon, toward Cap Bon, and perhaps only the sea remembers the submerged worlds.

In this handful of earth there was once shouting and fighting, there was pain, and a silence of the dead. He thinks again of Job, who will never be buried; Job blown apart. He knows that it is all far behind him now, and as he reaches for the statue in his pocket, he feels the dead watching him. Job is here. And others, too. People he met. People he killed. But that doesn't stop him. There is something stronger, more harmonious, than that. He thinks of Mariam, who gave him this statue. And he knows that she would understand what he is about to do. Mariam, who has traveled with him and who, at this very moment, is on the far shore of the Mediterranean, at Sidi Bou Said, all the way at the top of the village, at the marine cemetery, on the little wall overlooking the sea. Something makes its way between them in this vestigial daylight. He takes out the statue of the god Bes she has given him, the statue that survived the digs and was handed down like a secret, the ugly, deformed dwarf god with his disproportionate penis who watches over humans and drives away evil spirits, he takes it out, he knows nothing about its history, not even what it means, he remembers what Mariam told him about the Apis bull during their night of lovemaking, the tomb of the sacred bulls, he remembers the column of blue vapor that emerged from the tomb for four hours once Mariette Pasha opened the door to the Serapeum, and it is as if the statue he is holding between his hands had the power to seal the holes in tombs. What escaped, back then—the polluted air of centuries; what was lost—the footprint of the last priest: it is as if the statue could set it all right again. He handles it with deference and sets it in the hole he has dug. The statue must tremble at feeling the earth again. Does it know that Egypt is far away? No. Because Egypt is in fact very near, just as Mariam in this moment is also very near, at the marine cemetery in Sidi Bou Said, and in the tranquility of the light falling gently, weightlessly, upon the earth. Does she know he is laying the statue in its hole? To him this is its purpose: to bury his shadows, and all the others, the shadows of the thousands who died at Canne della Battaglia. At last there is a god to watch over them, the dwarf god who used to be placed beneath the head of the deceased to calm them and keep anguish at bay. He is burying the statue there on the hill at Canne della Battaglia, and they all feel relieved. Hear our defeats. He is burying it there so that it will watch over the Gauls from the front line who did not yield, and over Hannibal who was poisoned; let the statue with its contorted hairy monster's grimace watch over Grant and

Sherman, the burned victors, and the hundreds of thousands of young men who would have no life. Hear our defeats. Let it watch over Khaled al-Asaad, too, the beheaded Priam. Assem is burying the statue and that is his way of proclaiming his own defeat, of giving it a name. He is not sad, it is something he does gently, serenely. We have lost. Not because we showed ourselves unworthy, not because of our mistakes or our lack of discernment, we have been neither prouder nor more insane than others, but we embrace defeat because there is no victory, and the decorated generals, the emblems whom society venerates so fervently, they agree, they have always known this, they went too far, they lost themselves for too long for there to be a victory. Hear our defeats. He is burying the statue but it could also be Mariam herself doing it, on the far side of this Mediterranean Sea that has seen so much light and so much blood. And actually she is doing it, with the long circular gaze she sends sweeping over the sea, she is burying the statue, she too is thinking about the man she once met in Zurich but who has been with her ever since, because he gave her these verses, "Body, remember . . . ," at a time when it was what she needed more than anything: the memory of the body's pleasure, the imperious necessity of remembering what we are, yes, pleasure in the face of barbarity, sensual delight and struggle, she is full of that night and, like him in that same moment, naked in the face of the immensity before her. They love each other. They are not in the same place, they cannot see each other, they are simply both looking out at the same sea, that Mediterranean of blood and joy where peerless worlds have been born, and they love each other. Never mind the fact that their story—unlike the others—began with their bodies and is being written backwards, now, in absence; she sees him, she knows that they carry the same defeat within themselves, the defeat of time causing us, gently, to yield, the defeat of our vigor, diminishing, vanishing. Hear our defeats. There is no sadness, she has not lost anything, nor has he. He leans forward, covers the statue of the dwarf god with soil, and the earth shudders with relief. Something has been restored. The statue will be there for centuries to come, incongruous, perhaps, in this soil plowed by the sword and peopled by skeletons, but he knows this is as it should be. He knows that Job is watching, that on the far side of the sea Mariam is among the steles at the marine cemetery in Sidi Bou Said, on the territory of the Empire that never was, because Rome swallowed it, burned it, caused it to disappear, but it remains all the stronger for it, and can be found whole again in the word "Carthage," which contains everything, Carthage, the glorious city that defeated oblivion despite the ashes, hear our defeats, they say it together, with a sort of sweetness and delight, hear our defeats, we were only human, there could be no victory, only desire, until the submersion, only desire and the gentle touch of warm wind on our skin.

All of Haile Selassie's words in chapter VII are quotations taken from the speech he gave at the headquarters of the League of Nations in Geneva on June 30, 1936.

The quotation from Cavafy is from the poem entitled "Body, remember." Translation Alison Anderson.

The quotations from Mahmoud Darwish are from the poems "In Praise of the High Shadow" and "We Will Choose Sophocles."

ABOUT THE AUTHOR

Laurent Gaudé is a French novelist and playwright. After being nominated for the 2002 Prix Goncourt with *The Death of King Tsongor*, he won the award in 2004 for his novel *The House of Scorta*.